BEST
GAY
EROTICA
2009

BEST
GAY
EROTICA
2009

Series Editor

RICHARD LABONTÉ

Selected and Introduced by

JAMES LEAR

CLEIS
PRESS

Published in the United States.
Cleis Press Inc., P.O. Box 14697, San Francisco, California 94114.

Printed in the United States.
Cover design: Scott Idleman
Cover photograph: Celesta Danger
Text design: Frank Wiedemann
Cleis logo art: Juana Alicia
First Edition.
10 9 8 7 6 5 4 3 2 1

For Asa,
forever Best

CONTENTS

FOREWORD

A soup seasoned with cilantro tickles the palate differently from a soup seasoned with garlic or a soup seasoned with ginger. Same basic stock, but a subtly different taste sensation.

That's the way it is with the *Best Gay Erotica* series: it's an annual serving of gourmet erotica, but each year offers a special dining experience. The individual stories aren't the same from year to year, of course, but a different flavor dominates—a chef's touch contributed by the judge who makes the final selections.

My function as series editor is to assemble a range of potential ingredients—about forty reprints and original writing culled from several hundred submissions and suggestions. Then the judge selects his savory "bests" from my spread of literotica delectables, determining the twenty or so lip-smacking and pud-whacking stories that make up the book. That's why each year's *Best Gay* differs in tone (and taste) from the others.

For example: Mattilda Bernstein Sycamore was judge for 2006; her gender-queer sensibility infused the book with stories embracing a broader spectrum of sexual self-definition than in other years. Timothy J. Lambert was judge for 2007; his taste was more sexually mellow—a different degree of hot. Emanuel Xavier was judge for 2008; his background brought a touch of Latin heat to the table.

And so it is this year with James Lear, the refined and filthy-minded British author of *The Back Passage*, *The Secret Tunnel*, and other irresistibly consumable erotic groaning-board feasts. I'll let his thoughtful introduction speak for itself about his choices for *Best Gay Erotica 2009*; he has definite opinions about what constitutes worthwhile erotic prose—the sort of distinct sensibility, from him and from the dozen other judges I've worked with since 1997, that gives this series its tang.

In his intro, James singles out one selection, about which he writes: "My jaw dropped." That would be Robert Patrick's original narrative poem, "Mass Ass," which I first sent off to a *BGE* judge in 2002, and a couple of times after that, too; it really, really worked for me, but judge after judge passed it over. Try, try again, I say, and this year at last it was just the morsel James was looking for. Like James, I generally find that poetry, as a rule—no matter how potent its imagery—seldom sustains a narrative well enough to deliver real erotic crunch. Luckily, there's an exception to every rule....

Also: every couple of years, I invoke an "editor's choice" prerogative, adding to the judge's selections a story I admired. This year it's "Knives," by Xan West—an edgy, sensory fragment that wasn't quite to James's taste. But it tickled *my* palate, as a representative of one of the more exotic erotic flavors within the genre of sexual prose. It's the last story in the book—think of it as a particularly potent after-dinner mint. Now, enjoy the fea—okay, that's enough of this extended dining metaphor.

Richard Labonté
Bowen Island, British Columbia

INTRODUCTION: GETTING THE JOB DONE

James Lear

Erotic fiction—seemingly the most transgressive and liberal of all literary forms—is (or at least should be) one of the most conservative. It sets out to do a job: get the reader interested, get the reader aroused, and get the reader off. If it doesn't do these three things, then, in my book, it isn't erotic fiction. It may be many other things, but if it's not primarily an inspiration to masturbation, it doesn't belong here.

I read a great deal of erotic fiction as a young man, in magazines and funny little pocket-sized paperbacks, and used it in precisely the way it was intended. The stories that worked for me then, and work for me now, are those in which there's a good balance between preliminaries and actual sex, and in which there is some crucial tipping point when the protagonists realize they're going to have sex. In terms of visual pornography, it's the bit when the men squeeze their swelling groins and hold each other's gaze for a little too long, just before the dicks come out. In literary porn, it's the moment when the protagonist thinks "Oh, my God…"—the moment just before the roller-coaster ride plunges down the first big hill. In gay erotic fiction, the element of doubt and surprise about the other party's willing-ness adds extra charge.

I don't like stories in which there is no setup, no seduction. I don't like stories that portray sex as something empty or violent or degrading; erotic fiction is supposed to make us feel better, not worse. I don't like stories in which the sex is inci-dental. It has to provide the rhythm, the engine, and the heart-beat of the story.

The short story is, in many ways, the perfect form for erotic fiction. It gives the reader one good wank; it follows the pattern of arousal (long buildup, powerful "Oh, my God" moment; short, frantic final phase, and possibly a bit of recovery and wiping-up time); it evokes one mood or kink that can be selected according to the reader's whim. In all literature, nothing is more robustly functional than the erotic short story. There is an actual physical outcome to show if it's succeeded. When it comes to erotic fiction, a good review in a newspaper is nothing compared to two or three sodden Kleenex.

Plausibility is a key factor in good erotic writing. When we're young, we dream up elaborate sexual fantasies that stand or fall by their verisimilitude. I can remember plotting wild stories about how the school caught fire, and the football captain was trapped in an upstairs room from which I rescued him, only to discover just how grateful he could be…. But much of my mental energy was expended on making sure that he could really be in that place at that time, that the logistics worked, that it could just possibly come true, particularly if I carried a box of matches at all times.

All the stories I have selected for this anthology are rooted in reality. They all recognize and respect the fact that sex is most exciting when it arises from the everyday. Some of them explore those eternal fantasy favorites—the changing room, the enclosed railway carriage, the doctor's consulting room—that will always be fraught with sexual potential. Others take essentially mundane situations—sharing an apartment, going to the laundry, washing dishes—and infest them with sex. All of them respect the reader enough to assume he knows that we, the writers, are providing a service. If a story can entertain or enlighten as well, that's great, but those included in this volume have one mission in mind—to help you, the reader, to a good orgasm.

It's unfair to single out any particular entry, but I feel I must say something about the obvious odd man out in this collection, Robert Patrick's extraordinary narrative poem, "Mass Ass." I'm not a great reader of poetry, and if someone had told me that there was a long erotic poem on the short list, I probably would have sighed and rolled my eyes. I read "Mass Ass" (as I read all the entries) with no knowledge of its authorship. From the very first verse, with its outrageous mixture of low-down doggerel and hifalutin' language, my jaw dropped. I was there, standing in the fuck line with the poet, thinking randomly, hilariously, about Catullus and the Greeks, occasionally reaching out to squeeze a convenient cock. I love this piece of work unreservedly and am hugely gratified to know that it's written by a man who can rightly be regarded as a hero of gay culture.

James Lear
London

THE CHANGING ROOM

Bradley Harris

Ridge City Mall is far away. It takes about two
hours to walk there, past long rows of evenly
spaced paper box factories, then around a few
tricky corners filled with crisscrossing, unexpected traffic. You then walk over a small
highway with a very narrow shoulder, past a
sickly sweet smelling Tootsie Roll factory and
a lone Pizza Hut, until you hit the mall itself.
Sometimes Kyle walked all the way there, but
today he was going to splurge, spend some
money, take the bus.

Kyle had three hundred dollars in his pocket.
For half a year he had stashed away the money
his parents gave him for lunch, hoarding it in
a heavy black box with a lock his grandfa-
ther gave him on an early birthday. The night
before, Kyle had counted all his limp and dirty

twenty dollar bills, feeling their texture with dreamy, absent satisfaction. Surely his parents had noticed his drastic weight loss, but they said nothing.

The people on the bus do not look at him. They are mostly old ladies, and if they aren't, they might as well be. It takes a while. Kyle thinks about what he wants to buy, things he'd be embarrassed to ask his parents for. Bikini underwear, for instance, in bright colors. Sexy clothes. Kyle wants to buy sexy clothes, tight clothes. Clothes that show he has a body. Kyle is very skinny now, but tight with slender muscle; he hasn't been eating lunch, but he's been working out all summer. Sometimes at night he goes into the backyard and strips naked. As he looks at his body in the moonlight, Kyle pretends he is being filmed for a nude scene in a movie. He is sure someone is watching him, but he doesn't know who. An older man, probably. An older man might want him.

After getting off the bus, Kyle went directly to a small clothing store at the far end of the mall. The store rarely had any customers. On his trips to Ridge City, Kyle always found himself drifting to this store because Joe, the manager, had actually started talking to him a few months ago. Joe was in his late thirties, probably, a little goofy looking, with glasses and big white teeth and slight acne scarring on his cheeks. To compensate, he apparently worked out every day, because his solid body was ostentatiously attractive, especially in contrast to his affable, plain face. Joe smiled when he saw Kyle come into the store, and he swung his heavy body lightly over the counter.

"Hey, kiddo," Joe said. "You gonna buy something today, or just look around?" he asked.

"Probably just look," Kyle said, barely able to look at Joe, walking ahead of him. "But I might buy something."

"What do you want to get?" Joe asked, as he stared at Kyle from behind.

"I'd like to get some underwear," Kyle said quietly, over his shoulder.

"Oh, really," Joe said. "What kind of underwear?" he asked.

"Um…I don't know. I thought…maybe…some bikini underwear?" Kyle hoped that Joe wouldn't laugh.

"Bikini underwear?" Joe tried to laugh but started to blush. Kyle turned around and hugged his skinny torso with his arms. Joe shifted his weight restlessly from one leg to another and stole a glance at Kyle's lower body from the front, whip-thin in tight blue jeans.

"Yeah. I saw this show on TV where the guy was wearing red bikini underwear, and I liked the way he looked," Kyle said shyly, his words tumbling out fast.

"Who was wearing it? What show?" Joe asked, his hands on his hips, leaning forward slightly, looking right into Kyle's shifting eyes.

"Um, I think it was an old episode of 'Melrose Place.' The guys are cute," Kyle said.

"Okay," Joe said. "Let me go get you what you want."

As Joe walked slowly to the underwear section, he was almost certain Kyle was staring at him. Joe smiled. He was turned on by the attention and touched by Kyle's need. Months before, Joe had sensed Kyle's loneliness, and he recognized it as similar to his own at an earlier age.

"Here you go, try these," Joe said, passing an underwear package to Kyle. He smiled and rubbed his big hands together. "They get good-looking guys to pose for those things, huh?"

he asked, cocking his head and sidling closer to Kyle.

"Yeah," Kyle said. "They're pretty cute."

"You know, if you turn the package over, you can see what that same guy looks like in the underwear from the back," Joe said.

"I know," Kyle said, too quickly. He looked mortified, and Joe patted him on the shoulder, placatingly. The brief physical contact gave Kyle goose pimples all over his bare arms.

"Don't worry, buddy. You don't have to worry with me," Joe said.

"Okay," Kyle said. His heart started to beat in his right ear.

"I like the guys on those packages," Joe said, confidentially, leaning in very close. "I spend so much time here by myself...it's cool to have pictures like that to look at. I almost feel like I know them." Joe suddenly felt he had said way too much. Kyle looked at the package and turned it over. They stared intently at the model, who was slightly turned to profile the tighty whities. The angle of the shot was quite flattering.

"He's got a nice butt, huh?" asked Joe.

"Yeah," Kyle said.

"A really nice butt. Tight," Joe emphasized, as he stared at Kyle's hips and the sweet curve in the back of his jeans.

"He must work out a lot to get it to look like that," Kyle said.

"When a guy gets older, you need to work at it a little more," confided Joe.

Kyle flipped the package back over. "These are small...are you sure they'd fit me?" he asked.

"You've got a really tiny waist," Joe said, staring straight at

Kyle's hips. Suddenly, he had an urge to pull Kyle's jeans down. He wanted to see this kid completely naked, make him bend over and show his asshole. This kid must be so tight down there...for a daring second, Joe wrapped his big hands around Kyle's waist, as if he were measuring it. "I'd say a small is what you need right now."

Kyle stood for a second, almost gasping, not yet processing the press of Joe's hands on his hips, before moving away. "Can I try these on?" he asked. "I want to see how they look."

"Well...you're actually not supposed to open the underwear before you buy it," Joe said. A thought struck him. "How old are you, buddy?" he asked.

"I'm seventeen," Kyle said, embarrassed.

"Really?" Joe asked. He started to inch away from Kyle. "I would never have guessed you were so...you don't seem that young."

"I know," Kyle said. "When I look at my face in the mirror, I see a thirty-five-year-old, or something." He stared at the floor and gulped.

"I wouldn't go that far," Joe said softly. He felt hurt, for reasons he couldn't explain to himself.

"Can I try these on?" Kyle asked, still staring at the floor.

"Okay, just for you," Joe said. "Here's the key to the dressing room." Joe pressed it into Kyle's hand. As Kyle was walking away, Joe suddenly said, "I bet you'll look really hot in them."

Kyle stopped in his tracks, then turned around quickly. "Yeah?" he asked.

"Yeah. Really sexy. You've got a nice butt yourself, kiddo, anybody ever told you? Sticks out a little bit. And I bet you don't work on it."

They were silent for a moment. Kyle waited for Joe to keep talking.

"You've firmed up from when you first started coming in here," Joe said. "You been exercising?"

"A little," Kyle said. "I use my dad's free weights."

Joes hesitated, started to turn away, then said, "Hang in there. You'll look like that guy on TV in no time."

A customer came in, a middle-aged woman with long blonde hair, and Joe went to see if she needed help. Kyle went into the dressing room and opened the underwear package. He took off his pants and loose white underwear slowly and stared at his body, which looked pale in the unflattering light.

Kyle took out a bright red pair of the bikini underwear and tried to put them on. They were too tight. Kyle got hard instantly from the pressure. He looked at himself in the mirror for a long time. He looked better and better as time passed.

After about forty-five minutes, Kyle heard a knock on the door. He felt like he was waking up from a deep sleep.

"Hey, kiddo, you still alive in there?" Joe asked.

"Yeah, I'm still alive," Kyle said, in a flat, speculative voice. His eyes shifted to the changing room door.

"How do they look?" Joe asked, trying to sound professional.

"They're way too tight. I think," Kyle said. He felt a flush of courage. "Do you think I could get your opinion on how they look?" he asked.

Joe wondered if he had heard him correctly. This kid was just so lonely, dying for attention. After a moment, Joe decided not to keep Kyle waiting. This kid was brave, he had to admit. Plus, Joe was so turned on that the rational part of his brain shut off. The job? Who cared, who cared about the boring job.

"Yeah, I'll take a look, kiddo," Joe said. "Open the door."

Kyle's heart thumped loudly in his ears, and he felt like he was going to pass out. He opened the door and stood as far away from the glaring overhead light as he could.

"Nice," Joe said, his eyes clouding over with lust; a hint of Kyle's dark pubic hair curled out of the top of the underwear waistband. Joe wondered whether he should continue, somehow, with customer/employee formality. But when he saw Kyle's anticipatory, bright-eyed face, he knew he couldn't.

"Turn around," he said. "I want to see you from the back. Like on the package." Joe's mouth was slightly open and he was nodding his head. He was beginning to enjoy the role of older guy/teacher.

Kyle turned, arched his back, and widened his stance slightly. He was shaking with pleasure.

"They're way too small, buddy," Joe said, softly, as he cocked his head to get a better view. "They barely cover you back there. Sorry I got you the smalls."

"You are?" Kyle asked.

A bit of silence.

"No...no...I'm not sorry," Joe said deliberately. "You look so hot. Like neutron hot." There was a long silence. Kyle stood for an eternity while Joe surveyed him from every angle, keeping his distance.

"Okay," Kyle said, finally. "Could you get me the mediums?" he asked, not knowing what else to say.

His trance broken, Joe said, "Yeah, stay right there." He turned and dashed to the underwear section. His palms broke out in a sweat as he ran back to the changing room. Kyle hadn't moved an inch. Joe opened the medium package and threw Kyle a red pair. They landed on the floor.

"Take the ones you have off and put those on," Joe said, closing the changing room door and locking it. Kyle flinched when he heard the door lock, and he stared at the package on the floor. "Bend over and pick them up," Joe said softly. Kyle did as he was told, and the top half of his butt popped out of the size small briefs. Joe licked his lips.

"Look at me," Joe said. Kyle shifted his gaze from the floor and turned around. Their eyes met. A connection was made, a strong connection, welded willingly by mutual smiles. The smile on Kyle's face was big and toothy, and it transformed his gawky appearance. All at once, for the first time, Kyle felt sexy, and he looked radioactively sexy to Joe.

"Take them off," Joe said softly, not wanting to scare Kyle. After a moment, Kyle stripped and stood naked.

Without missing a beat, Joe said, "You're beautiful."

Kyle's smile got wider and he felt blessed. He felt as if he were going to cry, too. He'd been so unhappy for so many years. This first taste of adult happiness was new to him, and it demanded everything he had.

"Turn around now, kiddo," Joe said, his lowered voice daring to edge this exchange into something smutty. "I want to look at your tight teenage ass," he said, fetishizing their age difference.

Kyle turned and Joe let out an involuntary grunt.

"Can I see you, too?" Kyle asked, tentatively.

Joe stepped closer to Kyle and stripped off his shirt, then his shoes, then his pants and underwear.

They weren't Joe and Kyle, finally, and they weren't in a dressing room in Ridge City Mall anymore. They created another location.

At last, Joe asked, "When are you eighteen?"

They both laughed, coming down to earth.

"Next summer," Kyle said.

Carefully, Joe asked, "Are you a virgin?"

"I don't have any friends," Kyle said, skipping the smaller point and arriving at the larger issue. Somehow, he felt he had permission to jump to what was important—he felt that this man would understand. "I don't really have anyone. I'm alone all the time," Kyle said. Then, he felt he had gone too far.

There was a pause. Kyle was in agony.

"You'll have me," Joe said.

All during the fall, winter, and spring of Kyle's senior year in high school, he walked to Ridge City and tried on clothes in front of Joe. White briefs, black briefs, sleeveless shirts, and jeans, lots of jeans. "You look so great in tight jeans," Joe said, running his eyes from Kyle's tiny hips down to his feet. Joe started giving Kyle tips on how to bulk up, and though the young man remained almost painfully skinny, by the spring his body had developed more definition.

Joe talked lovingly about every little change and improvement he saw in Kyle's body, and he talked and talked about what they were going to do on Kyle's eighteenth birthday. Hypnotically, Joe would murmur detailed, fantastically dirty things he was going to do to Kyle, always coming back tenderly to what he was going to do to Kyle's "tight little teenaged ass." The repetition of this phrase grew more powerful each time Joe said it.

Kyle would constantly interrupt and say he wanted to do all that *now*, but Joe would shake his head and say, "We have to wait until you're legal, sweetie. You can wait, can't you? Let's go over some of the different positions we're going to use…"

Kyle would stare at himself in the mirror as Joe stared at him. Most of the time, Joe brought in clothes, leaned against the door, and half whispered instructions to Kyle, spiked with lurid commentary. Kyle was ordered to turn and stretch and bend, to hold strange and difficult poses. "We have to train that cute little body of yours," Joe said. "It has to be flexible and ready to take cock. That's all you're gonna do, is take cock. I'm going to fuck your tight little teenaged ass *every single day*."

"You are?" Kyle would ask.

"Every single day," Joe would repeat.

"Yes, Joe," Kyle would say.

"On your eighteenth birthday, you're going to take my dick."

Kyle smiled happily and put his arms around his savior.

One day, a month before his eagerly awaited eighteenth birthday, Kyle asked, "Would you try on clothes in front of me?"

Joe smiled. "You want to see me do that?" he asked.

"Yeah, I want to look at you again," Kyle said.

Joe went off and got himself a pair of small-sized blue jeans. He came into the dressing room and slowly started to take his clothes off in front of the mirror. Kyle was dazzled, and Joe was proud of his strapping body.

"This is yours," Joe said, running his hands down his body and then grabbing his dick.

"Mine," Kyle said.

It took Joe a while to get into the jeans. When they were on, Kyle went to Joe and kneeled down. Joe took Kyle's head and rubbed it deep into his crotch, then leaned back into a wall and let out a contented moan. Joe looked at them in the mirror and smiled at Kyle's fresh young nakedness, crouched over awkwardly, worshipping his maturity and largesse. They stayed in this position for such a long time that it felt to Kyle like he was not quite there anymore, like he was looking at himself in a movie on television.

Finally, Joe pulled Kyle upright. "You're so sweet," he said. "You'd do anything I asked, wouldn't you?" Kyle nodded eagerly. "You'd even give your tight little teenaged butt to an old, ugly fat guy if I told you to, wouldn't you?" Joe asked. "I want to see the oldest, nastiest, fattest guy come right in your sweet little face," he continued. The sound of a customer finally broke up their scene. Kyle left in a hurry.

On his eighteenth birthday, Kyle walked all the way to Ridge City for the first time in weeks, in the tightest blue jeans he owned; underneath he wore the red bikini underwear he had bought on their first day together in the changing room. When he got to Joe's store, Kyle stood and blinked, over and over. The store was gone, closed; boarded up and abandoned. Kyle's hands broke into a sweat. He ran around the mall, the ugly, boring mall, hoping to see Joe. He wondered if he could ask anybody what had happened to the store, but he knew no one there, only Joe.

For an hour or two, he walked around jerkily, trying not to cry. Finally, he sat down in front of the bus stop, and he did cry. He cried for all the years of waiting. He cried for feeling like the most rejected reject. He cried, at last, for no reason at all. An old lady lumbered up to him and, without saying a word, offered him a Kleenex. He sat next to her on the otherwise empty bus all the way home. As his stop neared, Kyle dried his tears a final time and murmured, "He liked me. At least someone liked me."

ABDUCTING FRODO

Jeff Mann

For S

He's even handsomer than I remember, striding out of Roanoke Airport's security area with his bags of luggage. Lean, rangy, shorter than me by several inches, younger than me by a decade. Boyish, with big, wide, shy eyes and a head of black curls. "My hobbit," and "Boy Frodo" I've called him for months, because of his amazing resemblance to Elijah Wood in *The Lord of the Rings* film trilogy. Just the sort to bring out the Top in me something fierce.

As the distance between us dwindles now to inches and the months apart shrink to seconds, as he moves closer and closer, I'm trying to look calm, in control, trying to hide the welling exhilaration I feel. Tonight his sweet young body has moved hundreds of miles through dark sky to me, from Manhattan, his home, and his husband, high over ocean and Pennsylvania earth, in and out of Dulles, and into these mountains at last. It's been a good long while since I've topped a boy this desirable, this smart and talented, this eager to be tied.

"Howdy," I mutter, gripping his shoulder with welcome. "Hey," he whispers, squeezing my forearm. I'd hug him, but, despite months of email flirtation, up to now we've just been writer and reader, men with mutual friends. We've never before been together like this—as soon-to-be lovers, as Top and bottom. Things are still careful, tentative. The hard hugs, the deep kisses, they'll wait till later, after I have him home, stripped, collared, and bound.

"The beard looks real good," I say, studying his smile, the angles of his face, the new stubble darkening his cheeks. That little patch of silver on his chin makes me want to kiss him hard right here, in the middle of the airport, under the disapproving, pious eyes of Southwest Virginia, but I don't have time to share fisticuffs with homophobes. I want us on the road and on the way to Hanging Rock Park and then on down the interstate to Pulaski as soon as possible.

We've been planning this weekend for a long time, plotting the details of his abduction, the way we'll meet, the ways he'll be restrained, what I'll do with him once he's my prisoner. It's been like composing literotica together. I've ordered him not to shave or use deodorant for days, because I love beard shadow, facial hair, and armpit musk. I've told him to wear his scruffiest jeans and, beneath them, a jockstrap. In my truck, as promised, wait the collar, the cuffs, the hunting knife, the tape, the bandana.

Our time is finally here. He grins up at me, and the difference in our heights maddens me, makes me want to rope and gag and fuck him, hold him and protect him from the world, which is, of course, exactly what he's come so far for. He studies me for a long moment, assessing the man he will soon submit to. In about fifteen minutes, for the first time he'll be exactly as he wants to be—completely helpless, a big man's captive—and I'm sure he's still a little nervous. I'm a little nervous too. He's come a long way, and I want to be the perfect Top, the perfect Southern host. I want to insure that all his fantasies, the many scenes we've discussed so long on email, come true without a flaw.

Novelty, anxiety, and anticipation: the combination's a true aphrodisiac.

What does he see? A tall, beefy guy with a close-cropped silvering beard, a black biker jacket, a black leather-flag baseball cap, faded jeans, and black cowboy boots. Would have worn the black cowboy hat, but it was too windy today. The mountaineer queer, I call myself. Too much of a country boy to tolerate cities, so I've had to make peace with my Appalachian hills, with the way they've shaped me. Luckily, I'm fierce enough to defend myself and my kind, if need be, from local fundamentalists and conservatives. Two hundred pounds and regular gym visits help.

I grab the larger of his two bags and nod toward the exit. "This way." It's 11:00 P.M., and I want us home as soon as possible.

"Good to be here, Strider," he says, following me toward the escalator. "Let me visit the restroom, and we can be on our way. No other luggage to collect."

Strider. I love it when he calls me that. Wish I resembled handsome Viggo Mortensen's Aragorn as much as my boy resembles adorable Elijah Wood's Frodo, but he calls me by

Aragorn's nickname anyway. He knows that Aragorn is a major role model of mine, that the ring I'm wearing tonight— silver dragons wrapped around a green stone—is a copy of Aragorn's, that I have replicas of Aragorn's ranger sword and elven hunting knife hanging on the walls at home. Surely he knows the name makes me feel strong, protective, a warrior of sorts. The kind of man I want to be: ruthless to enemies, tender and caring with friends and kin. Pretty much the kind of man I already am, after years of conflict and self-shaping. Surely he knows that he's entirely safe here, that a boy who submits to me will be shielded from the hateful orcs of this world, protected from all pain except whatever abuse he begs for.

On the escalator, a little polite chat. "How was your flight?" "What's the weather been like down here? Any snow predicted?" In the restroom, urinals side by side. Then we're out in the darkness together, heading across the huge parking lot toward my pickup truck. The wind gnaws at our necks. A few dead leaves scuttle by. One day I'll be decrepit, but I'll have this night to remember. I'll have written what I could to retain what I can.

Six months since we met by that pool in New Orleans, introduced by mutual friends at Saints and Sinners, the LGBT literary festival. Five months since our email correspondence began, after he'd read my *Masters of Midnight* vampire novella *Devoured* and some of my other BDSM-themed work. He was particularly excited by a short story I'd published in the online magazine Velvet Mafia. "Captive" is about a young Southern man who gets picked up, overpowered, bound, gagged, and used by a Yankee biker and loves it so much he eventually decides to become the man's full-time slave. *How much of that story was true?* Frodo asked.

How often do you live what you write? he wondered. *Have you ever been part of a consensual kidnapping? Have you ever kept a guy bound and gagged for hours? After reading "Captive," I really want to submit to a man that way. Do you know any trustworthy New York City Tops who might introduce me to bondage?*

Perpetual Southern altruist, I offered my kidnapping services, agreeing to play out with him some version of "Captive," if he could ever get out of that noisy Northern city and down to my mountains for what we soon began dubbing "A Wilderness Bondage Weekend." His husband gave reluctant permission and took to calling me "Wilderness Daddy." Mockery, perhaps, but it was a title I gladly embraced. My husband bought me both Aragorn and Frodo bookmarks and plans to return from a business trip tomorrow in time to join us and help create a Hobbit sandwich.

Months of sweet planning, and now here we are. I shove Frodo's luggage into the truck's extended cab, then turn to him in the dim parking-lot light. I have to touch him now—I'm tired of waiting—so, awkwardly, briefly, I stroke his curly head. So soft. I can't wait to feel his mouth on my cock, taste his nipples between my teeth.

"Look what I wore for you," he says abruptly, pulling up his knit sweater long enough to show me his T-shirt. BOY is the slogan printed across his chest. "Very good," I say, chuckling but secretly touched. I open the passenger door, he slips in, I close the door behind him. We both know that this is where it really begins.

Behind the wheel now, looking around the parking lot to see who's within eyesight. A fat middle-aged man—well, about my age, I guess—trundles by with his rolling suitcase, so I wait till he moves off before I look Frodo in the eyes and say, "Ready?"

"Yes," he whispers, meeting my gaze for a second, then dropping his eyes.

My beat-up old black-leather backpack is behind the seat. I pull it into my lap, unzip it, and begin sorting through what's necessary.

The collar first. A short length of heavy chain to circle his neck and then padlock together just below his clavicles. The metal's chilly, but soon enough his young heat will lend it warmth. The molecules will speed up the way my heart is speeding now.

"Looks good," I say, stroking his hair. "You're mine now, right?" As we've agreed, he'll remain collared till I return him to this same airport three days from now.

"Yes," he says, looking up at me long enough to nod, then lowering his gaze back into submission. How much I love a boy's submission. Nothing gets me harder.

Well, I guess one thing gets me harder: restraining and gagging a boy. The gag, unfortunately, has to wait. Right now, we both know, it's time for the cuffs. Eagerly, without waiting for my order, he holds out his hands before him, and I snap the black metal around his wrists. I'd prefer to cuff his hands behind his back, but he's a novice at all this, and it's a good hour to Pulaski. I want him powerless but not hurting. Not yet, anyway.

That's all for now, simply because I have to pay for parking first. I toss the extra sweatshirt I've brought for this purpose across Frodo's lap, concealing his cuffed hands. I tuck the slave collar under his sweater. I drop the backpack on the floor between his feet.

"All right?" I ask. He nods. I start the truck, turn off the blaring country-music radio—107.1 FM, my favorite station for backroads driving—let the engine warm up for about half a minute, then head for the brightly lit booth on the lot's far edge.

"How you?" I ask, passing the elderly attendant a dollar.

"Jus' fine," he replies. "Not a bad November we're havin'." He and I have to shoot the shit briefly—we mountain folk make a short social chat out of every interaction. His accent is about the same as mine, and I'm guessing he likes the same kind of music and food I do—Toby Keith and Reba McIntire, brown beans and cornbread—but I'm also guessing his values are otherwise pretty different. This is the sort of queer juxtaposition I love, the sort of irony I relish, created as it is by the contrast between appearance and reality. I look and sound and sometimes pretty much act like just another local redneck in a pickup truck, and in many ways I am just that. But of course I have a leather-flag sticker on my rear window and, this blessed night, a handsome young man from New York City collared and cuffed in the passenger seat. I guess I've become the kind of wildly contradictory and complex man I've always been attracted to and I've always wanted to be: good baker of biscuits, collector of cowboy boots and hats, aficionado of four-wheel-drives, adept user of cuffs and ball gags, deft maker of knots. When you're butch enough to blend in, you can get away with a hell of a lot in this region, despite the stupid fuckers that compose the Religious Right and run most of Virginia.

So, on out to 481, then Interstate 81, nothing much said. Another five minutes down the interstate, and we're in the tiny park beneath Hanging Rock Mountain, the place I've picked out well in advance for its darkness and isolation.

I pull into the gravel lot, gratified to see that no one else is parked there. As I'd hoped, it's a little too late, a little too cold, for teenagers to be necking. Nothing to see but the looming blackness of mountains, a hillside of bare trees across the road. No sound save for the distant, just-audible purl of a creek. Civil War battle here a long time ago, men fighting for power. No fight tonight. One man's more than ready to give up power, one man's keen to take it.

"Ready for Part Two, boy?"

Frodo nods. Since midsummer I have been waiting for, dreaming of, jacking off to the thought of what I'm about to do next.

The Case XX knife was a gift from my high school biology teacher, the lesbian godsend who helped me come out. She presented it to me just before my first deer-hunting foray with Mike, my hot straight buddy, whose hairy chest and black beard I so quietly admired, whose easy mountain masculinity I tried to emulate. Tonight, after decades of whittling the occasional twig and otherwise lying unused in my series of pickup trucks, ready to threaten or slice any assailant if necessary, it serves a rich purpose.

I slide the blade out of its black sheath and hold it up in the starlight. Frodo stares at it, I stare at him. At the same time that he knows that I would never harm him, I hope he's sweating just a little. Later, when he's naked and hog-tied and ball-gagged on my bed, I may have to run the knife ever so carefully over his nipples, neck, belly, and cock, just to hear him gulp and whimper.

The edge is a mite dull, got to admit—will have to sharpen it later. But, with just a little effort, it slices clean through the black bondage tape I ordered from San Francisco's Mr. S. With one hand, I carefully slide the knife back into its sheath; with the other, I hold the segment of tape, about eight inches' worth, a lustrous cross section of darkness, by one end in the air between us. "Keep still," I say. Frodo gazes quietly at me, then nods, closes his eyes, and settles back into his seat. Slowly, gently, I center the tape over his mouth, then smooth it across his face.

"Fuck," I grunt, sitting back to admire him. My cock, fairly hard since I first saw Frodo in the airport, is swelling considerably larger in my jeans. "I have been wanting to see you this way ever since I met you," I can't help but groan. "Nothing prettier than a good-looking boy with his hands bound and his mouth taped shut." I reach over, press the tape against his face a little closer, study the indentation of his lips beneath the shiny black, savor the contrast between the smooth gag and the rough stubble on his cheek.

These are my aesthetics. These are the sights and sensations I live for. Don't know why, don't care why. Why question blessing?

Blindfold next. I pull the black bandana from the backpack, my last prop before we get home to the big bed and the heavy bag of toys I'll be lavishing on Frodo all weekend. His dark hair's so thick I fumble for a little, but finally his eyes are covered and the cloth's knotted behind his head. He leans back into the seat and into helplessness. I've taken away his speech and his sight and the easy use of his hands. All he can do now is relax into the darkness. All he can do is relinquish.

"My little kidnap victim," I growl, patting his knee. "You look so fucking fine. You're looking as sweet as that poor little boy who got all roped up in 'Captive.' You set?"

Frodo takes a deep breath and slowly nods.

"You like this? You like being bound and gagged?"

Another nod. Palpable enthusiasm.

"Cuffs not hurting you?"

Unhesitating shake of the head.

Some bottoms might prefer a less solicitous Top, and I can be brutal, callous, and indifferent if they want that, but my natural tendency's to check on a captive's comfort with great regularity. When a boy's given up his will to me, that means his fate and his fantasy are in my hands, and I want to make sure he's where he wants to be at all times. Part of the code of Southern hospitality, I guess.

I study Frodo for half a minute, listening to that distant creek, exulting in how hot and handsome he looks with metal around his wrists and tape across his mouth, wanting to memorize what details I can to cup like water in the face of any future drought. Now I'm unbuttoning the fly of his jeans, and, yes, as promised, there's the pale gleam of white jock, the feel of its coarse fabric beneath my fingers. That's our luck, his and mine, that hard lump I grip and squeeze gently inside the jock and knead till my boy groans. I lean over, gratefully kiss his forehead, then pull up his T-shirt, slide my hands over his smooth, flat belly, up to the little hillock-swells of his chest, to the few curls of hair between and around his nipples, to the nipples themselves, just about my favorite part of a man, soft and hard at the same time.

"These are gonna be sore as hell by the time you leave. You want that, right? I'm gonna be sucking and tugging on these all weekend. I'm gonna worry 'em like a dog."

"Umm mmm." Frodo nods, arching his chest against my fingers, then begins a soft little moan as I dig my fingernails in just a bit. Goddamn, how I cherish the whimpers a boy makes against a tight gag.

I give his right nipple a final pinch, then start the engine, slip in a CD for the hour's drive south, and turn back toward the interstate.

We're not a mile down 81 before Frodo lifts his cuffed hands over his head and slips them behind his headrest as if I'd bound them there, then slides down in his seat till his arms are stretched tautly above him. Note for future reference: this boy, unlike many nervous novices, might relish a little discomfort and might benefit from very secure restraint. Later, after I've stripped him down to his jock, I'll have to rope his wrists good and tight to the headboard while I eat his ass. Maybe buck and gag him while I fix us breakfast tomorrow. He's young and lean enough to endure a few lengthy sessions and challenging positions, and he's going to look mighty pretty drooling around a fat black ball or thick bit.

Almost midnight now. The dark hills and pastures are streaming by, the lights of trucks are blurring past. I wonder if the sight of a man being kidnapped is giving any of these high-seated truckers huge hard-ons. For a moment, I worry that someone with a cell phone might call the cops, then mutter "Fuck it" and turn the music up louder. I'm forty-six: *Carpe diem* is a timely motto.

The CD's one of the latest by hot, handsome, hairy, goateed Tim McGraw, my favorite country music star. Talk about a man I'd give my soul to kidnap, strip, rope and gag tight, then keep captive and top continually, with alternating brutality and tenderness, for about six months to a decade. In his plaintive tenor, Tim's singing "Set This Circus Down," and I'm pounding out the song's rhythms on Frodo's knee, quietly exuberant, delighting in the rasp of fiddle and dwelling on all the previously-agreed-upon pleasures to come.

It will be so sweet to finally get my boy naked. How fine his armpits will smell and taste, and a fucking rapture to rope his hands behind him, spread his legs and eat his hole, to wake him up, after a drowse together, with my cock up his ass, ride him on his side, on his belly, my big bear weight growling on top of him. I can tell I'm going to be entirely besotted by his ass. On his back then, his legs over my shoulders, our eyes inter-locked while I ride him hard. So many varieties of tit clamps and gags to use, the music of muffled pleas, and tape across his chest, pinning his arms tight to his sides, layers of tape around his wrists and ankles. Pissing over his head and shoulders in the shower, knotting a piss-soaked sock in his mouth. Cooking him barbeque tomorrow, getting him good and drunk, tying him to a chair and feeding him with my fingers, cornbread and coleslaw and bourbon-barbeque ribs, letting him lick sauce off my fingers and my beard.

In his mute and blind cocoon, Frodo, I suspect, is dreaming of the same things, all we've promised one another. That quiet young stranger by the guesthouse pool last May, chatting with his husband on a cell phone, looking up at me with an inter-ested smile—who would have guessed how desire's electric language and serendipitous switchbacks would lead him here? What a gift, when greed meets greed and one man's longing completes another's.

The CD's ended. I drive awhile in silence, occasionally looking over at him stretched out in his seat, slender and curly-headed as a captive Bacchus.

"Comfortable?" I ask. He's so still I wonder if he's dozing.

"Umm mmm" is his quiet reply. I recognize the serene tones

of complete surrender, the ripe calm of orchards before harvest, of high-grass pastures before the scythe, the calm of appetites certain to be sated.

"We'll be home in just a little while," I say, squeezing the hard jock, tracing the imprint of his cockhead with the side of my thumb. We're hurtling along at seventy miles an hour, yes, the hard, deadly pavement and the hillside's rocky soil only feet from us, but I have to touch him, his lean and fragile body, again and again and again. Soon enough our weekend will be over, our long-awaited idyll will be ended. So, keeping careful eyes reluctantly on the road, I stroke his belly, play with a nipple. I fondle that endearingly silver-stubbled chin, caress the curls on his temple, rub his mouth's glossy seal. Tenderly I trace his eyebrows, the line of his jaw, then rest my hand soothingly on his thigh. For the time being, his life is mine, his warmth pulses beneath my palm. Tonight, our fates and brief bodies move together, intertwined through autumn and the dark. Tonight, one hand on his body, one hand on the wheel, I'm threading black hills with consummate care.

TWICE DICKED

Landon Dixon

A fitting end to a shitty day—my boyfriend getting cock-whacked.

I peeped at him and his bum-buddy from behind the tinted glass of the sliding doors that looked out onto the swimming pool. Kent, my Kent, and some badass biker type were bobbing up and down in the deep end, swiping tongue like Winona Ryder swipes clothing.

The guy aggressively probing Kent's tonsils had a big bald head, a two-tone Texas goatee, facial and earrings, and enough tattoos to cover two normal-sized bodies. The blazing sun set the water to glistening on his sunburned cinder-block shoulders and head as he frenched my lover like he was fluently bilingual. I slid a damp, shaking hand into my jacket pocket and gripped the butt of the gun I sometimes kept there.

The barrel-chested tough guy stuck his thick, pink wedge of a tongue out, and Kent sealed his lips around it and began greedily sucking up and down its slimy length like it was a hardened cock. Then the dude with the 'tude shoved Kent back, lunged over to the edge of the pool, hopped up onto the side, and spread his legs. He gripped his hard, bent-to-the-left cock and gestured at Kent with it. My trembling index finger coiled around the trigger of the gun, testing the tension.

"Come and get it, cocksucker!" the tattooed behemoth with the shaved hard-body and beard-matching black and blond bush yelled, his huge, pink body gleaming under the glaring sun.

"Sure, Brick!" Kent enthused in his sweet bottom-boy voice, his baby-blue eyes lighting up with desire as he watched the nasty man fist his hard-on. He glided over to Brick like a serpent glides into an oasis, slid in between his muscled thighs, and encircled Brick's rigid, purple-helmeted dick with his long, slender, manicured fingers. He began tonguing the bloated cocktop, expertly and familiarly swirling his slippery, pink pleasure tool around Brick's massive hood.

"Fuck!" Brick and I grunted, he in ecstasy, me in agony.

Brick ran his stubby fingers through Kent's long, blond hair, Kent gripping the stud's quads and mouthing cockhead like the seasoned snake charmer he was, tugging on Brick's mushroom cap with his full, red lips. Brick closed his wild, ring-fringed eyes and moaned like a wounded animal. I flicked the safety to OFF, and my finger danced along the slick, curved edge of the trigger.

Kent inhaled more of Brick's bent boner, sensuously but relentlessly sliding his lips down the angry erection till pert nose met hairy balls, till he had Brick's tool embedded in his mouth and throat. Then he pushed out his tongue and licked at the man's big balls.

I squeezed the butt of my gun like I meant to throttle it, jacking my rage and courage to the firing point, willing myself to jerk the gun out of my pocket and end this daylight nightmare. I stared bitterly, hungrily at Kent and Brick, at Kent looking into Brick's eyes and disgorging half of the ballsy biker's cock, then chugging it down to the roots again. Kent repeated his wicked sword-swallowing over and over. The sight of my guy deep-throating another in the sparkling, sun-splashed water was burning my eyes and frying my brain.

The heavy muscles on Brick's rugged arms and shoulders suddenly locked up, and I knew he was only seconds away from blowing his load, blasting my once-and-no-future boy-toy's mouth full of his sizzling seed. No man could endure Kent's awesome cocksucking for long. Kent knew this better than anyone; he broke free of Brick's clawing fingers, spat the man's dripping, inflamed dong out, and drifted away.

I loosened the grip on my gun, then sheepishly pulled my hand out of my pocket and stared at my twitching digits. It didn't take a PI to figure out that this was far from the first time for Kent and Brick. And if that was the way Kent wanted to play it, then that's the way he could have it. But he could count me out of the game. I might not be the most honest dick who ever pounded pavement or pucker, but I damn well knew right from wrong.

I looked out the window again and saw that Kent and Brick had climbed out of the pool and onto the diving board. Kent stretched out on his back on the narrow, pebbled surface, like a lion in the sun. He had a slim, bronze, well-toned body, with large dark nipples, long supple legs, shapely succulent feet, and an elegant, arrow-straight cock. He lifted his legs and spread his cheeks, exposing his smooth, pink hole to Brick, inviting the hell-raising hunk to punch his ticket.

Here's to you, Kent, you fucking slut! I thought, and almost screamed, as I unzipped my jeans and yanked out my cock. I was hard, and growing, and I angrily polished my pole while watching Brick crawl over to Kent, roughly grab Kent's legs, and stab his cock into Kent's asshole.

"Yes!" Kent shrilled.

I fisted my dick full blown and steel hard, my hand and mind a blur, filling my eyes with the raw, sexual sight of the two nude and lewd men cocking on the diving plank. They weren't cheater and cheatee anymore; they were just two sun-baked studs, one of them hammering his hard cock deep into the inflamed chute of the other, putting on a man-show for me.

My hand flew up and down my prick as Brick savagely pounded his heavy dong in and out of Kent's warm, gripping butthole and Kent frantically hand-pumped his own swollen organ. I shrugged off my jacket, tore open my shirt, and pulled and pinched my engorged nipples, tugging on my cock while reveling in the hard-core, he-man butt-fucking taking place right in front of me.

The diving board rocked up and down in rhythm to Brick's violent anal assault. I torqued my hand up another notch, to keep pace with the sweat-smeared dude's powerful, churning hips; his bold, rippling ass; his plunging cock; and my balls tightened ominously in prelude to blastoff. And that's when Brick's gigantic body started jerking like a puppet on a string. He threw back his head and let out a roar that cleared the fences and ricocheted all over the neighborhood, pouring white-hot cum deep into Kent's stretched-out sexhole. Kent screamed at Brick to fill his bum with boiling semen, even as he jerked jets of jism out of his own cock.

My legs quivered like skyscrapers come the Big One, and I grunted with pleasure, spraying thick sperm onto the glass and carpet. Brick's built-for-shit-disturbing body spasmed over and over, the wild man obviously dropping a humungous load into Kent's sexual core, as Kent pulled frenziedly on his own dick, jacking creamy jizz over his sun-kissed chest and stomach.

The bad boys came and came hard, and so did I. And I didn't bother cleaning up the mess I left on Kent's window and floor.

When I got to the office the next day, a woman was waiting for me. She was a joyless-looking dame of around forty, and a round forty at that, with close-cropped, mouse-brown hair, dull, gray eyes, and a chubby face bottomed by slablike lips. She was wearing an ill-fitting business suit and no makeup, her one concession to femininity being a couple of small, silver earrings, which she kept in her nostrils.

"You Clark Tozer?" she demanded.

"Yeah," I replied, ushering her into my inner office.

She got to the point. "I want you to catch my husband screwing another woman."

"Uh-huh. And what's your name—and his?" I said, trying to hold back the bored expression seeping into my face like piss into a paper towel. Fifty percent of my caseload is cheating spouse, forty-nine percent insurance fraud, and one percent interesting.

"My name's Mrs. Bethel Wojakowski-Gutierrez," the woman said with practiced ease, "and my husband's name is Steven."

Apparently, Bethel didn't give a good goddamn how Steven was caught cheating, just as long as he was. "You want me to set him up?" I asked.

"I want you to get evidence of him screwing...cheating on me with another woman," she repeated, the no-nonsense look never leaving her plain-jane face. She had all the charm of a bulldozer, and was probably just as effective.

"Why?"

"You get paid to annoy your clients, or to do what they tell you?"

"A bit of both," I replied, folding my hands in my lap, leaning back in my chair, and smiling. "I've got a passive-aggressive personality."

Humor was as wasted on her as cock on a clitoris, and she wasn't standing for any Q&A, either. She pulled five one-hundred-dollar bills out of a small bag roped around her beefy shoulder and said, "You get these when I get the pictures." Then she stowed the cash back in her bag and pulled out a photocopy of her husband's driver's license and one of his business cards, tossing them on my desk.

She had a vendetta. I had a client.

Steven Gutierrez was an architect, worked in a towering, silver-glassed building downtown. And it was well past ten by the time he finally strolled into the parking lot, jumped in his Pacific Blue Jag convertible, and raced away into the night. I followed him, parked a couple of cars away when he eventually pulled up in front of a trendy, strip-mall bar, as his wife had predicted. He leaped out of his luxury car and strode inside.

I turned to Shawneece, my partner for the night, and told her it was time to go in search of the most dangerous game.

I'd used her on a number of other equally sleazy jobs, and although she was a little too street for sophisticated Steven, I was confident that her big, brown eyes, tits, and rear-end would carry the day.

"Paradise Motel on Kirkland, right?" she said, sliding her plush bottom out of my car and almost out of her leopard-print skirt.

"Right. Room Seventeen. The one with the curtains that don't close all the way." The night man and I had an arrangement.

I watched Shawneece's jiggling buttocks as she tramped through the oak door and into the bar. Five minutes later, I was watching her jiggling tits coming the other way.

"He don't like girls," she said, once she was back in the car.

"You sure?"

She looked at me; gave me a sad, knowing smile. "A lady can tell, honey—and so can I."

"Well, uh...okay," I mumbled, pondering the possibilities. "Twenty bucks for your troubles, okay?"

I dropped Shawneece off at her favorite street corner and then drove back to the bar. Betheldozer hadn't mentioned anything about her hubby not liking cunty, but as I dredged up a mental picture of the missus, I sure as soft-on couldn't blame the guy. I decided it was time to take matters into my own hands.

I walked into the bar, and a half hour and two drinks later, I walked out with Steven Gutierrez. He was raring to go rearing, and I knew the place, so to the Paradise Motel we za-zoomed. And while Steven was getting more comfortable and horny in Room Seventeen, I was working a deal with Fuckflop Farley, the soul-patched semiliterate who manned the check-in counter come the midnight hour. He would handle the infrared camera on the outside, while I manhandled the cocky cheat on the inside.

Steven was lying on the bed dressed in nothing more than a shit-eating grin when I got back to the room.

"You don't waste any time," I commented, admiring his creamy-white, muscular body; his pink, protruding nipples; his thick, uncut cock. He had a handsome, dimple-chinned face, and his dirty-blond, shoulder-length hair and big, blue eyes reminded me of Kent. My cock grew as hard as the City with the memory, and the stark-naked reality.

"You're wasting time," Steven said, his dick twitching with desire.

I doffed my duds and jumped on top of him, covering his hard body with my body, rolling my stiff seven-incher over top of his pulsing erection. I hungrily attacked his mouth, chewed on his rose petal lips, jammed my tongue in and plowed it up against his. And as the forty-something flamer joyously fought back with his own crafty tongue, I thanked my lucky stars that the well-paying job had become both personal and professional.

We heard something rap against the window—fuck-up Farley juggling the camera, or his prick, too close to the action, no doubt—but I diverted Steven's attention by pumping my hips, dry-humping the sweet-smelling hotty as we urgently frenched. We pressed lips, hips, tools, and tongues together for a torrid while longer, and then I licked and bit the hard-breathing hunk's ears and chin and neck and brought my mouth down to his nipples.

"Yes!" he groaned, fumbling with a name I hadn't given him, his buff body undulating as I wet-kissed his nipples.

He ran his fingers through my short, jet black hair, then threw his arms up over his head and abandoned his oh-so-edible body to me. I swirled my tongue around first one engorged nipple, then the other, before closing my mouth over his left nip and sucking on it, tugging on it, biting it. His blossomed buds were obviously supersensitive, because he whipped his head back and forth on the pillow and moaned long and loud as I tongued and mouthed this one.

The foreplay had gone on long enough. It was time to eat meat—big, thick, cum-oozing meat. I swung around on the creaky bed-of-a-thousand-grunt-and-groan-sessions so that my knees straddled Steven's head, so that my numbingly hard cock dangled dangerously just above his open mouth, and his own hardened member was in my hands, up against my lips.

I swarmed kisses all over his bulbous cockhead, slurped slime from his yawning slit, my lust ablaze. I excitedly stroked his throbbing dong with one hand while I juggled his furry balls with the other, and he gave as good as he got, engulfing the tip of my pulsating pole in his warm, wet mouth and pulling on it. He gobbled up more of my cock, then got the good old sucking rhythm going, moving his head up and down as I pumped my hips, his mouth and tongue sliding easily back and forth on my dick; his hot, humid breath steaming around my saliva-slick shaft.

"Fuck, yeah, baby, just like that!" I yelped, before spitting on his meat and rubbing the wet into his foreskin. I earnestly hand-cranked him, while I popped his swelled-up hood in and out of my mouth, breathing in his ballsy scent, my head spinning and body shaking with the delightful smell and taste of him—and with the man-made miracle he was working on my dong.

We stroked and sucked and tongued each other's flaming cocks for a good, long, wet while in our mano-a-mano sixty-nine position, until I felt my cheeks being spread apart and a wet mist hit my itchy butthole. The damp feeling was quickly replaced by a far better feeling—Steven's fingers sliding into my chute. The guy obviously came prepared, and I was always prepared to cum.

"Yeah, finger-fuck me, baby!" I screamed, as Steven sank two of his digits into my man-catcher and continued to suck on my cock.

I rotated my tingling butt on his fingers, reveling in the sinful sensations his impudent pokers and pouty lips were eliciting. He slammed his fingers knuckle-deep into my gripping, dripping bunghole, filling me up, then began plowing my ripe anus with his digits. My body got all hot and heavy, my legs trembled out of control, and I struggled to maintain my mouth-hold on his dick, as the pretty boy banged away at my backdoor and spanked my cock with his tongue.

"I'm gonna cum!" I shrieked into his penis, all too soon. I frantically churned my hips, fucking his mouth like he was fucking my ass. Then I was jolted by fiery, all-consuming orgasm.

My cock exploded and I rocketed sizzling semen deep into Steven's mouth and down his throat, my sweat-dappled body coursing with sexual electricity. I blasted that well-hung horndog full of my rubbery man-goo, and he swallowed as much as he could, all the while valiantly bum-fucking me with his fingers even faster than I could spurt spunk down his gullet.

When I finally calmed down, I refocused on Steven's unfulfilled need, and with his digits still plugged into my butt and wiggling around, I again attacked his lovely cock with my mouth and hands. I slapped his shaft and knob with my playful tongue, sucked up and down on his prong, his foreskin sliding along with my lips, and squeezed and fondled his balls.

"That's it!" he hollered in no time at all, and his cock pulsed hot, salty cum into my sucking mouth, just about drowning me in his jizz.

I gulped as fast as I could, ecstatic to receive a much-needed protein shot which served to salve some of the bitter feeling from my breakup with Kent. For the first time in a long time, I left work that night with a good taste in my mouth for a change.

I slapped the full-frontal glossies of Steven and me onto my desk in front of Mrs. Bethel Wojakowski-Gutierrez.

"What's this shit?" she bleated, tearing my triumph asunder. "I wanted pictures of Gutierrez fucking a woman! Not another fucking guy!"

"Yeah, but…this is even better, isn't it? I mean, you can really discredit—blackmail—your husband now," I spluttered.

"He's not my husband, shit-for-brains! You believed that story just because we share a last name? You idiot! I'm as queer as folk! Steven Gutierrez is my opponent in the State Assembly election! In the Laurel Heights district—the one with the huge gay and lesbian population! I'd heard he was dabbling in heterosexuality, and you were supposed to prove it—to discredit the bum!"

I gaped at her fat ass as it stormed out of my office, along with my five-hundred-dollar fee plus twenty dollars for expenses. Politics was an even dirtier business than the gumshoe racket. First by my boyfriend, then by my own cock: I'd been dicked two days in a row.

Someone was going to pay, I mused bitterly—someone had to pay. A certain heart-stealing, sword-swallowing, blond-haired bottom boy instantly sprang to mind. My thoughts—and dick—hardened. Kent—my Kent—was about to get the sweaty throat- and ass-reaming of his life.

TEMPORARY

Tulsa Brown

"Listen," I said, "I'm going to take these heels off."

The dishwasher looked up. He was short and broad, dark as French roast coffee, muscles hard as an iron gate.

"I don't give a shit, man."

He laid a hair's emphasis on the last word, maybe to let me know he wasn't fooled by my red satin dress and the oak-brown hair that swept past my shoulders. Yet I distinctly remembered him looking when I'd waltzed from the dressing room to the club's little stage, a few hours ago. His head turned so fast his vertebrae crackled.

And he was still staring. I slipped off one pump, then the other, dropping five inches to the kitchen's cool floor. The man was taller than me now, and I felt the vertigo thrall of fear and excitement. I loved to be looked at but I couldn't read his steady, nailhead eyes. I'd guessed wrong before. Terribly wrong.

I set the black patent shoes on top of the stainless-steel counter, spiked heels lined up, weapons if I needed them. It was 3:00 A.M. and we were the only ones left in the place. The dishwasher snorted and turned back to his work. I braced myself for my own—scraping and sorting. It was hard to imagine that a few hours ago people had been whistling for me, hooting and stomping on the floor, and now I was scraping their half-chewed food into the garbage. My stomach roiled. *Show business*, I thought with a grimace.

"How come you're doing dishes if you're a star?"

The words jarred me. The man's lip lifted on the edge of a sneer.

"Well, it was a charity event. Everybody pitches in. The others waited on tables and took tickets."

"But you got this."

Laughter lurked under the words. My hand went to my hip. "Yes, I did. And guess what, Einstein: tonight I'm going home and I'll never have to see this shithole again. I bet that you do—every single day."

His nostrils flared. "It's just temporary."

"So was income tax!"

For an instant we glared at each other. Then he seized an arm-breaking tray of dishes and hoisted it over to the sink, biceps straining his kitchen whites. I turned with an abrupt flounce, breasts swaying. I'd been performing with four others over the last six months, doing drag shows for charity benefits and the occasional gay bar gala. We usually worked for tips, but on bad gigs—like this one—we had to "assist the staff," too.

"We're making our names," Carl, our MC, said over and over.

"I already have a name," I'd snapped at him. "And if somebody doesn't write it on a check real soon, I'm dumping this trailer-park talent show."

"Trailer park!" Carl snarled. "I've done Vegas!"

"So I heard—on your knees."

I thought he'd smack me, but his eyes suddenly narrowed. "It's not a bitch contest, darling. There is no prize."

That's when I started getting the crap jobs, yet he didn't dare cut me loose. I was a singer, a torch. The others only lip-synched, but I really sang, steel-note cries of longing that pierced the smoky haze. Up on the stage, blazing like a satin flame, I could hold the entire room in my palm—the men's desire, the women's envy. And in that instant my feet didn't hurt, and the four hours of shaving and waxing didn't matter. The bit of flesh strapped down tight between my legs no longer existed. I was Ashley Laine, a woman flying, not falling.

I won in other ways, too. When Carl walked out into the crowd, to fluff up interest and stroke a man or two, everyone laughed. That's because he looked like what he was—a hefty TV squeezed into his aunt's castoffs. He was six foot two in flats and wore a thrift shop Doris Day wig. Pure plastic.

I was different. I strolled into the audience like a long-legged sylph, and the air sizzled. Tonight I'd put my foot on a big man's chair, between his legs, the patent leather toe just millimeters from his bulge. He was a burly trucker type, the kind who swore he'd never come to a place like this. In the dazzling glare of the spotlight, I let the red satin slide to the top of my thigh. I could hear his excited, quickening breath, feel his eyes scour my body—nipples, naked leg, my succulent painted lips.

He was enthralled. I drank Carl's envy from across the room.

There is a prize, darling, I thought.

A clatter of pots made me turn. The dishwasher was still at the sink, jaw set, big shoulders moving with the precision of anger. Frayed male pride. I was sorry for what I'd said.

"What's your name?" I called over the noise.

He didn't look up. "What the hell do you care?"

"Oh, don't tease me. I know I've been naughty."

The last word caught him by surprise and he glanced over, grinning in spite of himself. After a moment he pulled out of the water and started toward me, wiping his hands on a towel.

Closer was better. His whole upper body swayed when he walked, a sailor's big-armed swagger that made me catch my breath. There were amethyst highlights in his sienna skin; his lips and big palms were startlingly pink. The part of me flattened by the spandex panties began to thicken.

"Tell me yours first," he said.

"It all depends. If you're not a cop or my mother, I'm Ashley Laine."

His smile broadened. "Rory Park." He thrust out his hand and enveloped mine, a dark nest enfolding a pale little bird.

I squeezed back. "It would seem there's a Park at the end of the Laine."

He laughed abruptly, surprised again, a flash of white and wet pink that gave me a flutter. Damn, this was looking good.

"So, if this career is only temporary, what are you on your way to?" I said.

"Oh." He pulled away. "There are lots of possibilities. I've got lots of prospects."

He began to wander through the narrow aisles, his back to

me. There was something about his knotted shoulders and the way he trailed his fingers along the stainless-steel counter that made my chest tighten.

"Are you on parole, Rory?" I asked quietly.

He looked back at me, chin tilted up, not exactly a dare. "You got a dick under that dress?"

My heart leapt into a trot but I held his gaze. "The last time I looked."

Rory smiled ruefully. "Yeah, me too. Last time I looked."

Great, I thought. *Another Mr. Right-cum-felon.* Yet I felt a strange sense of relief. This was the kind of news I usually got late in a relationship. Way too late. I turned to my dirty trays again and dove into the task with brisk energy. Finish up. Go home. Wang off if you have to.

But Rory didn't go back to his sink. He settled across the counter from me, leaned forward on his arms in a hard-sculpted, masculine trapezoid. "Hey, you're really something, you know? If I saw you on the street, I never would have guessed. I'm not queer or nothing, but you're pretty hot."

I should have kept my mouth shut, but he'd jabbed at an old, tired wound.

"Guess again—I'm not gay, either."

"What?" He pulled back, then grinned. "Ah, you're shittin' me."

I straightened, flushing.

"Here's a telegram for your thick male brain: It isn't always about sex. It isn't about what you stick where and into who. I'm a female who happens to have a male body—for the moment. You understand temporary, don't you, Rory?" I flipped my long hair with a toss of my head. "I'm not in drag, I'm...in process."

His gaze dropped to my breasts, to the bullet-firm nipples pushing against the silky fabric.

"So those are yours?"

He reached out—he was going to squeeze me like cantaloupe. I smacked him away so hard my own hand sparkled with pain. His eyes widened, a dark flash of lust and anger, and my heart leapt. I thought he might grab me across the counter.

Bang! Bang! Someone pounded on the heavy metal kitchen door, the one that led to the alley.

"Richard! Are you in there?" a voice called.

Oh, god. The voice skewered me like an icicle. "Don't open it," I said.

Rory glanced at the door, then at me again, bewildered.

"Richard, don't screw with me, bitch! Carl nailed you. I know you're in there."

I reeled with the nausea of betrayal. I'd made some mistakes in the past, and I'd been running from this one for months. And Carl knew it—that asshole!

"What the hell is going on, Ashley?" Rory hissed.

"Don't do anything. I'll check for another exit."

I hiked up my skirt and sprinted away, dodging around the club's tables. I reached the front door and yanked on it. Damn! It could only be opened with a key. By the time I was back in the kitchen, Rory's hands were on his hips, his broad chest puffed with anger.

My ex was kicking at the door now, a terrifying rattle. Thank god it only opened from the inside.

"The front's locked," I panted.

"Look—does he pack a gun?"

"Not...always."

"Shit!" Rory whammed the counter with the flat of his hand and the dishes jumped. Bad news. My ex renewed his assault on the door.

"I know you're in there, you lying slut!"

Rory shot me a hard look. This wasn't his fight or his problem.

"All right. I'm calling the cops," I blurted.

I was almost into the hallway when he seized my arm.

"No—please." His eyes were large, liquid, frightened. "My parole is in another state."

The revelation opened inside me. If the police showed up, Rory was the one going to jail. Yet he wasn't threatening me, he was asking. It was a strange sensation to have this big man pleading with me.

"But what am I going to do? If I walk out of here, I won't get home." I could hear the shrill, desperate note in my voice. "And if we don't get rid of him, someone else will call the cops."

Rory hesitated, then held a finger to his lips. Shh. He strode back to the metal door and wound up and hammered it with the side of his fist.

"What the hell are you wailing about, man?" he roared.

There was a second's stunned silence. My ex wasn't expecting that deep basso.

"I'm looking for a bitch named Richard. Someone told me he's in there."

"That nut in the dress? I sent him home an hour ago. The most useless piece of shit I ever had in my kitchen."

The pain was swift, a boot in the stomach. But Rory held up his hand to me—hold on.

"Well, just let me in to check," my ex said.

"I open this door and my balls are breakfast. Staff only."

"You've gotta come out sometime." The threat was dark, rumbling, a storm I already knew.

"Yeah, I do," Rory called. "But I hope you brought a chair, man. I'm night crew. I don't walk for another five hours."

Silence. I twisted on the hook, fingernails digging into my palms.

"Fuck." The word was a low thud of defeat, the last stone pitched backward by a man leaving. For long seconds Rory and I were transfixed, straining for more sounds, but there was nothing. At last I exhaled, a rush of relief like the air from a punctured balloon. I backed against a wall and slid down, bones melting. I put my hand over my face, eyelashes trembling against my palm. Don't cry, don't cry.

Just another day at the office, I thought bitterly. Betrayed, threatened, terrified. And for what? So I could stand on a stage for three minutes and feel...real? All I wanted was someone who understood the woman I was going to be and yet desired me now, too. Instead, I found lovers who loathed themselves for wanting me. I felt like a wineglass, a toast you drank, then smashed in the fireplace.

"What was the name of that song you sang tonight?" Rory's voice was soft.

I looked up, blinking tears. He was back at the sink, washing quietly.

"'Skylark.' It's an old jazz tune."

He nodded without looking at me. "It was beautiful. Sad but beautiful. It pulled me right out of the kitchen. They wouldn't let me out front to watch, but I stood in the hallway, listening."

The surge of gratitude almost closed my throat. In that

instant his few words meant more than the waves of applause that had rolled out to me under the spotlight. It kindled an idea that pulled me to my feet.

"Rory, why don't you take a break? Go sit down at a table, relax for a bit." He turned. I was leaning against the wall, head tilted back, my bare neck arching out toward him. At last a slow, smoky smile lit up his handsome face.

"All right."

I gave myself three minutes in the dressing room to brush my hair and freshen my makeup. On impulse, I peeled off my stockings, and the rich, smooth fabric of my dress caressed my bare thighs as I moved. Anticipation ran over me like waves of champagne. I stepped into my high heels again, and the sudden lift straightened me, thrust my silicone breasts forward. The dark-eyed siren in red who gazed back from the mirror was a flame. A torch. Some people might call this a fantasy, but it was my deepest truth.

Rory hadn't turned on the lights. The spillover glow from the hall swept out over the empty tables in a soft, dreamy wash. He'd lit the candle on his table and sat upright in the chair, dark hands on his white, uniformed thighs. Anxious. Peeking from behind the partition, I took a breath to slow my pounding heart, then stepped out of the shadows and began to sing.

"Well, the men come in these places, and the men are all the same…"

The long night had rasped my voice to husky velvet, and I softened Tina Turner's "Private Dancer" to a lullaby. Each stride a slow undulation, my long, pale legs emerging through the slits of the skirt, then retreating. A tease. I let my elegant, gleaming nails skim the surface of the polished tables.

Rory's gaze was rapt, devouring. I meandered toward him, exhilarated by the desire I could feel radiating from his body. When he reached between his thighs and squeezed the bulge, longing leapt beneath my dress.

I'd reached him at last and slid my ass onto his tabletop. The flickering candle lit up the sheen of sweat on his throat; his eyes had the glaze of a dream. I settled a foot against his thigh, the spiked heel indenting the muscle, and crossed one leg over the other, close enough that his warm, quick breath whispered over my naked knees. He closed his hand around my ankle, then leaned forward and opened his mouth on my bare calf in a soft, wet bite. Desire twisted the song in my throat to a moan.

He stood to embrace me, and I spread my knees wide to receive him, still perched on the table like an ornament. He opened my mouth with a demanding kiss, entered me with his tongue. I sucked on it eagerly, wanting to take him inside me any way I could. When his thick fingers began to creep under my panties, I edged away, afraid to ripple the surface of his fantasy. He pulled away from my lips and panted lightly against my ear.

"I want to see you—your hard-on and tits. I want to see it all."

I prickled with apprehension. I'd never done this for anyone, not in a dress. "Close your eyes first."

Rory took a step back, grinning faintly, and did as he was told. The hard jut in his white pants made my mouth swim. I slipped off my underwear, and my erection surged to full height, a slender rapier bobbing under the weight of the swollen bell cap. I gathered my skirt back and let it cascade down both sides in a satin waterfall. When I gently stroked myself, the tingling rush was amplified. Dizzying. The feminine fabric against my skin and the big-boned male in front of me were a potent cocktail.

"All right," I said.

Rory opened his eyes. For a second he just stared, eyes darting from my face to my breasts to the erection I still tugged between my legs.

"Oh, girl," he breathed. "You're so fine."

Oh, girl. The words ran through me in an electric current. I squeezed myself, my cockhead surging in a sweet throb on top of my delicate fist. Rory unzipped, clumsy with want, fumbled with his shirt and sent a button sailing. It rolled in a spiral on the ugly burgundy carpet. Then he gathered me up and swept me down to that carpet, too.

He was vast, dark, undulating—a powerful wave of a man. I was the red sunset dancing on his surface. On the club floor between the tables, I lapped at his chest and sucked hard on his nipples, feeling his low, hungry sounds vibrate against my lips. He touched me with a rough, workingman's awe, as if he were afraid he might break something.

"It's my real hair," I said. "You can pull on it."

Emboldened, he wrapped the silky length around his fist, tight enough to make my scalp burn. But it wasn't pain—as soon as he stepped into a wide-legged stance in front of my mouth.

His cock was an angry, plum color, a swaggering brute that twitched toward me, taut and urgent. I licked the underside of the fleshy ridge, teased the satin surface with my teeth. Rory growled deep in his throat and urged me forward, his fist at the base of my skull. When I opened my mouth to take his full length, he thrust forward and stretched me wide.

It was like being entered—deep, thrilling, necessary.

I gripped both his thighs for better balance, and he pushed one of my hands away.

"No, work your dick. Ride it, baby. I want to see you come."

I didn't need a second invitation. I flipped up my skirt again, and we fell into an extraordinary rhythm, pumping like a machine with two pistons. He bucked into my mouth, and I rode my own familiar grip, stoked by sensation and the thick, guttural sounds of his pleasure. My own rushed up quickly, churned in my balls in exquisite curls. I gripped my cock around the base, stalling.

Rory was driving faster, harder. Every time he hit the back of my throat, the impact hurtled down through me and throbbed between my legs. He was fucking my whole body through my mouth. Just as I wondered how long I could hold off, he yanked my head back. His cock pulled out with a soft slurp, my mouth hung open in a surprised O.

"Come!" Rory blurted.

The jets struck my bare chest like hot cream, pulse after pulse that snaked down into my cleavage. The triumph released me—my own bliss caught me in that instant, a low thunder that pulled a cry from my center. I clung to his thigh and rode one galloping wave after another, spasms twisting me, wrenching me with joy as I shot far out between his legs.

The floor was hard and it didn't matter; we floated on a languid stream. I lay in the crook of his big arm and watched the faint flickering of the candle against the ceiling high above. A corner of my mind nagged at me: Rory's record, his broken parole. But I refused to worry about it tonight. Happiness was the most temporary thing of all.

"I guess I owe you a dress." Rory touched the stains below my neckline, which were already starting to stiffen.

"The night's not over," I said. "It could be two."

He laughed, a single happy note that gave me courage. I rolled onto my side and nestled my cheek against his chest.

"What made you want me?" I asked softly. "Seeing that you're not queer."

Rory took a breath. "Oh. Because you're beautiful and you looked so alone."

"We're all...kind of alone, if you think about it."

He hesitated shyly. "Nobody ever sang for me before."

I heard the words yet felt something else beneath them, as delicious and intimate as a squeeze. *Oh, girl.*

I fluttered my fingernails down his chest in a teasing, butterfly trail. "And she just might sing for you again."

DON'T TOUCH

Jamie Freeman

I thought for a moment it was him, ducking
out of the men's room on the main concourse,
about twenty paces ahead of me. Even after
a decade, I see him sometimes, in New York
coming out of a restaurant that serves only rice
pudding, in London in that bookshop across
from the National Gallery, in Budapest in line
at a McDonalds, and now, ducking out of a
men's room in Salzburg after midnight in a
blowing snowstorm. Those same dark features,
the same short muscular build. I imagine I can
see the thin nose, the small perfect hands, but
now I am surely succumbing to the lure of
memory. I imagine him turning to take another
look at me, then, seeing who I am, he will drop
his bag and his coat on the platform and fly
into my arms. We will hug like Ilsa and Rick

would have in the Paris train station if the world had been a simpler place. But films, like life, have a way of making the simple complex and nurturing our bitterness, and Ilsa will always leave Rick standing alone on the platform. And the man coming out of the men's room does look at me, light eyes touching mine for a moment too long, but then he hurries down the corridor in the direction of the trains. And it is not who I thought it was.

I stop off at the men's room for a piss, the sad sound echoing through the empty tiled room, then make my way to my train.

It is nearly 1:00 A.M. by the time the train starts rolling north toward Berlin and I am ensconced in an otherwise empty compartment, long coat tucked around my shoulders, legs propped on the seat opposite me, thinking of him. I lay aside my copy of Isherwood's *Goodbye to Berlin*, flip out the overhead light, and stare into the cold night.

Grove was perfect. And I'm not just saying this because he was my best friend and my first love. He was one of those people that everyone loved, everybody wanted to be with and, for a time, he was mine. And he made me feel special, winking at me when people said stupid things, touching my shoulder when we stood together listening to a new song on the radio, rubbing his leg absently against mine in our favorite booth at the deli near our apartment. He was so alive, so physically entrancing. *No wonder people love him*, I used to think. No wonder, when he moves like that, body sinewy and graceful as a dancer, small and solid with muscle. He would sometimes stand next to me on the Metro, when the train was crowded or when he was too keyed up from the movie we'd seen to sit, and his arm would be wrapped around the pole, small hands grasping the smooth metal like a lover. I would watch his arm muscles flex with the slowing of the train as we approached each station, the ropy vein sliding along the pale inside of his forearm, and I would pray that we would somehow never reach our destination, that we could somehow ride on in this hot compartment forever, my throat dry and full of my desire for him, his hands wrapped around the cold chrome pole. But our stop would come and he would look up and smile at me and I would be pulled along in his wake, out the doors, through the turnstiles, and up the towering escalator into the night.

The first time I saw Grove naked, we had been out to one of the clubs in the southeast dancing, Tracks, probably, and the men had circled him like jackals while I watched him dance alone or while I danced close myself, brushing my hands protectively against his sweaty mesh shirt and listening to him laugh and sing along to the music. Our bodies crushed together that night like they never had before, and I felt certain that this was the night he would pull me into his bed and begin things with a kiss.

But when we staggered back into our apartment, and we were roommates once again, he was talking about Lucy, his girlfriend, whom I reluctantly loved, who was in Boston visiting her parents this weekend.

"God, Chris, I love her so much," he said, pulling his shirt over his head, muscles aligned in an inverted triangle that pointed to the thicket of pubic hair that peeked out the top of his loose jeans.

I pulled off my own shirt silently and watched him kick off his shoes, feet pale and perfect against the dark carpet, toes digging into the shag as he stretched again and again. I couldn't bear it any longer when he reached for the zipper of his jeans, and I staggered drunkenly into the bathroom. The shower was biting cold and it sobered me somewhat, flushing the alcohol and the cocaine and the desire down the drain in swirling circles. And I stood there for a long time under the icy rush.

"Fahrkarte, bitte," a voice startles me and light suddenly floods the compartment.

The man is tall and plain, cheeks a little too full, stomach a little too heavy, but he has the Austrian precision of dress and he is smiling as he holds out a gloved hand.

I hand him my ticket, which he punches and hands back to me. *"Gute Nacht,"* and I am again in darkness.

"Bitte, ist hier frei?" Another voice says even before my eyes have fully adjusted to the darkness. A tall backlit figure with a large duffel bag on his shoulder stands in the doorway.

"Genau," I say, *sure,* pointing to the empty seats across from me. The stranger comes into the compartment, stows his bag on the overhead shelf, and pulls a paperback book out of his coat pocket. He drops down on the seat opposite me, props his feet up, and leans his head back against the headrest. His eyes close as his head touches the cushion, and I think again of Grove and that night after the club.

I was in the shower for what seemed like a long time when I heard him open the door. "You're gonna waste all the hot water," he said, padding across the room and flinging open the door to our standup shower stall. "You," he said, grabbing my arm, "out." He pulled me onto the bathmat and stepped past me into the shower, our bodies colliding for an instant, the hair of my chest brushing against his shoulders, the tip of my cock sliding lightly along the top of his buttocks. "Jesus, Christopher, it's fuckin' freezing," he groaned. Then he flipped the hot water on in a swift sure motion, and pulled the door shut behind him.

I've thought about that moment a lot over the years, as though it was a moment of great import, a moment of potentiality, but I think now it was a moment of drunkenness and misplaced desire. I stood there for a full five minutes, cold water dripping off of me onto the fuzzy bathroom rug and the old orange bathmat, and I considered just opening the door and stepping back into the shower with him. I watched him soap himself, hands running along the muscled planes of his legs, reaching up between them to the dark triangle that was obscured by the steam and the textured glass of the shower door. But I couldn't get past Lucy and history and, finally, defeated, I left the bathroom, soaking wet, and climbed into bed, burrowing under my comforter and wishing myself into oblivion.

When I woke the next morning, Grove, in a pair of my boxers, was sleeping next to me. He was lying on his stomach, snoring slightly into the pillow.

I reached out and grabbed his shoulder, shaking him awake. "What are you doing here?"

"*Bitte?*" The response is from the man opposite me in the train car. I realize I have spoken out loud.

"I'm sorry," I say in English. "I was dreaming."

"No problem," he says, smiling and shifting slightly in his seat, his crossed legs resting next to mine.

"You're American?" I ask.

"*Genau*," he says, laughing.

We talk for a while, laughing and recounting travel stories in the dim confines of this train compartment, hurtling north through the snowy night. There is a sliver of moon and, when the train reaches higher ground, it occasionally makes its presence known, light sliding across the man's lap, his arm, the stubble on his chin. He is animated, with hands that tell more of his story than his rumbling voice cares to, but he wears a gold band on his left hand, barring my way to more intimate discourse.

We lapse into silence after a while and I watch him shift in his seat, searching for a comfortable position to sleep in. His long legs stretch next to me, rolling against me as the train turns, then rolling off me as the train shifts direction again.

I was the best man at Grove's wedding. He and Lucy were married on a cruise ship somewhere off the Pacific coast of Mexico. Lucy and I planned the wedding on the living room floor of the apartment I shared with her fiancé, watching "Mad about You" and leafing through glossy magazines. To our twenty-year-old sensibilities, it seemed the most romantic thing in the world to be married in a simple shipboard ceremony. We pictured the three of us standing with the captain in his dress whites at the railing overlooking the sunrise and the Mexican Riviera. But by the time Lucy's mother had wrestled control from us, it became a lavishly produced affair involving more than three hundred seasick guests crowded into the *Acapulco* ballroom.

The first thing Lucy's mother did was to find out the name of the travel agent and demand that the couple-to-be be split up. So, for the three nights prior to the wedding, Lucy roomed with Genie, her maid of honor, and Grove bunked with me on the far side of the ship.

We spent the first two nights of the cruise drinking and dancing, and Genie and I ended up passed out together in an oversized queen-sized bed in her room while Grove and Lucy slept in mine. But the night before the wedding was different for some reason. The traditional last dance at the disco was an old Sinatra version of "Almost Like Being in Love." Genie and I had just stepped out onto the floor, her skirt flaring up as I flicked her to the end of my arm. She laughed and twirled back to me, but then Grove was there, tapping her on the shoulder and bowing formally, asking to cut in. I stepped back and held out Genie's hand to him, but he took my hand instead. Meanwhile Lucy bowed to Genie and the two of them danced around us in lazy circles. Grove and I danced close, his chest pressed against mine, and he laughed and breathed alcohol onto my neck.

"You're the best friend I've ever had," he said, "I hope you know that, hope you know I'd do anything for you." And my stomach fell through nine decks to plunge into the ocean.

We did a couple of Jäger shots with the bartender after the girls went back to their room, then did a couple of lines of coke before we stumbled back to our cabin.

"I can't sleep with her tonight, Chris," he slurred as we staggered down the corridor. "It's my last night being single, you know? And I just can't do…"

He lurched as the ship slid to one side beneath us, caught himself on my shoulder then righted himself and pushed open the door to our cabin.

"Coffee," he whispered, so I called room service and, within minutes, we were sipping hot creamy coffee together on the tiny sofa. Grove drank a cup and a half of coffee, then staggered into the bathroom. He was gone a long time.

"You okay?" I asked, knocking gently on the door.

There was a long silence, then he opened the door and looked out at me. He had washed his face and straightened his clothing.

"You look better," I said.

"I feel better. I'm sorry—Christ!—you shouldn't have to babysit me."

He pushed the bathroom door open a bit wider and walked out, remarkably steady. He turned back around and looked at me with eyes so full of emotion that I wanted to run away.

"I love you, man. I could not do this without you standing beside me every step of the way. I'm terrified. I mean, my god, I'm getting married tomorrow, I mean today, man. I...I don't know what I would do...you mean so much to me. You're my best friend in the world."

He had this indescribably mournful look in his brimming eyes, and all I wanted in that moment was to hold him so close to me that he would feel safe and loved and a little less terrified, so I reached out a hand across the distance to touch his chest and he stepped back, quickly, deliberately.

He must have seen the shock on my face because he said, "No—you don't understand. It's not what you think."

And I stood there and looked at him, still and silent.

He watched me with those green eyes of his and I felt dizzy, a moment of déjà vu that hit me with such force, I stepped back and sat on the foot of the bed. And he took a step back from me and landed on the sofa.

We sat there facing each other for a long moment.

"It's not what you think," he said again.

"What exactly, am I thinking?" I asked, angry or hurt, cheeks flashing red.

He stared at me for a moment, then I felt his eyes slide through me into the far distance. "I think," he said from behind those dreamy, unfocused eyes, "I think sometimes I want one thing and then sometimes I want something else." His eyes snapped back to me, fast, startling me. "I'm not afraid of you."

"I know that," I said, slightly disoriented.

"There are lines, Christopher. Lines between things, between this and that..." his voice trailed off and he ran his fingers through his hair. "Lines that divide what we do and who we are from what we don't do and who we're not."

"Grove, I wasn't trying to—"

"Oh, I know," he said, waving his hand dismissively. "I know you weren't doing anything, it's just that there's a line. Here. Tonight."

I watched him in silence, feeling the distance opening between us like a sudden chasm.

"And I've already made my decision about who I am and what I'll do. I mean, I'm getting married tomorrow—"

"Look, Grove, I'm not trying to do anything here—"

"I know, I know," he said again, his voice quavering for a moment. He spotlighted me with those eyes again, boring into me. "This is about me. I'm the one standing on the edge."

I locked eyes with him for a long time, waiting for this moment to pass. But it did not. We sat, staring at each other across two feet of beige carpet, across the greatest divide that can ever separate two people. I loved him. And I was completely immobile, knowing that if I moved a millimeter, I would leap across the chasm into his arms and this moment would end with one of us walking out the door forever.

But then he startled me, reached down and pulled off first one shoe, then the other.

"No words," he said flashing me his nervous smile.

He kicked his shoes toward me, then reached up to unbutton his shirt, tan fingers moving slowly from top to bottom against the white cotton, unhooking each button then moving on to the next, pulling the tails of his shirt out of his pants, then taking the shirt off and tossing it over the back of the chair next to him. He peeled his tight T-shirt up across his belly, his abs, his hairy chest. He pulled it over his head then threw it to the side.

I could feel the pressure of my erection poking through the alcohol-soaked moment, rubbing against the inside of my boxers.

He looked at me for a long moment, and I didn't dare breathe until he leaned forward and reached down to peel his right sock slowly from his foot. He let his fingers trail along the naked arch, flexed his toes, grinned up quickly at me then peeled his left sock off as well.

When the socks were off, he stood up and began to unbuckle his belt.

I stood up and reached out to help him, but he caught my hands in his. He pushed them back toward me and said two words: "Don't touch."

And suddenly I understood.

On the train I feel the incremental slowing of the braking systems that signal the approach to a station. Along this part of the route, the stations are little more than a platform and a ticket booth, standing in the middle of a cluster of ten or fifteen buildings so, less than five minutes after the train coasts to a stop, we are under way again.

I look across at my companion, who appears to be asleep, and I see the impressively long, thin outline of an erection against the denim of his jeans. The jeans are tight enough, and his ardor bold enough, to see the contours of the head outlined like an invitation.

I shift uncomfortably in my seat, pulling my coat over my own lap and my own rearing erection. I am not wearing underwear and the friction feels like the tickle of flames along my shaft.

And I think again of Grove, standing there less than two feet from me, unbuckling his belt and watching me with those eyes. He tugged on the belt, pulling it away from him, the leather holding on to each belt loop for an instant until he finally ripped it free in one broad movement, brandished it in the air like a whip, then flicked it across the room.

He pulled his pants down to his ankles and stepped out of them in a swift motion, then stood back up, the only thing now between my raging erection and his about three seconds worth of white cotton and about two feet of empty space.

He stood for a moment, then grinned foolishly and crossed his arms, tapping his foot in mock exasperation until I began to pull off my clothes in a flurry. When I was down to my underwear, I took one look at him and pulled them down to my ankles, kicked them away from us and stood completely naked in front of him, my erection bobbing and bouncing between us.

He looked up and down my body for a long time, his eyes beginning at my feet and traveling up my muscular legs, across the planes of my thick, toned thighs, and into the dark tangle of hair that clustered around my balls. He looked carefully at my cock and for a moment, I could feel the shadow of his regard across the length of my shaft. I shivered involuntarily, drawing his focus up to my face.

He had this look on his face that I had never seen before, a look of desire and humor and something else, something like resignation.

He grinned again and dropped his underwear, kicking it to the side.

I drew in a quick breath and concentrated on not touching his cock as it bobbed in front of him. I had seen it before, but not quite like this. It was short, but thick, with a pale shaft that extended to a particularly thick purplish head. The head was straining like a creature trying to escape the tiny cluster of pubic hair. His balls were large and heavy, hanging low in their shaved pouch.

Grove reached down and gave himself a couple of strokes, a left-handed grip that was loose and exact at the same time, a practiced move that made my cock jump in response. He grinned at that and began to rub his abdomen with his right hand, pumping with one hand and, with the other, rubbing circles along his belly then his chest, circling his tiny dark nipples for a moment then sliding back along his treasure trail for a two-fisted massage of his cock.

I watched him rub himself and reached down with my right hand, pulled lightly on my balls, slid my fingernail down the length of my cock, enjoying both the sight of him touching himself and the feel of my own gentle solo prelude.

He started stroking himself more rhythmically, eyes roaming across my body as if he was storing every contour, every muscle for later recall. He reached up absently and spit into his hand, slid the spit along the hot length of his cock, rolled the saliva across the head with the palm of his hand as though he were chalking a pool cue. I smiled at this, spit in my own hand and mirrored his movements.

We stood there stroking ourselves and watching each other, our movements synching as the heat began to build in my stomach. Suddenly, in an instant, his eyes snapped shut, he shuddered, and then came in a torrent, globs of searing hot come hitting my stomach, my legs, my toes, and the carpet between us.

He looked supremely embarrassed and uncomfortable as if he did not expect this to happen, or was chagrined by the speed with which it did.

I let my hand slack off, but when he saw my erection bobbing there, he said, "But you didn't come."

I shrugged. For a moment, he looked as though he would drop to his knees and take my cock into his mouth. This thought sent a pulse through my cock and, seeing my continuing excitement, Grove stood up, turned around, put his feet together, and bent himself at the waist, palms stretched out against the floor in front of him. "Don't touch," he reminded me as I moved behind him.

I dropped to my knees behind him, my face hovering less than a foot from the spectacular sight he had just thrust at me. His limber body doubled over on itself, thrusting his asscheeks up and apart, and there, buried in a damp wisp of hair, his rosebud sphincter stared out at me. It pulsed slowly in an odd, sentient pattern and the hair around it trembled slightly under my breath. He shifted a fraction closer and it was all I could do not to plunge my tongue into him, but I kept just enough distance between us to keep from touching and I grabbed my rearing cock with renewed vigor. The musky odor of him was sweet and rank at the same time, drifting across the slight divide and invading my senses as I pumped myself faster and faster. I breathed deeply, licked my hand, and stroked myself. I groaned in spite of myself, breaking the silence awkwardly, like a tourist in a foreign library, and I endeavored, in spite of my growing excitement, to memorize the line of fur that ran along the very innermost crevice of him, the tantalizing scent of him, the tiny purple sphincter that winked its carnal code at me. And I stroked myself, my breathing becoming ragged, catching in my throat. Heat rose off my cheeks in waves, and I felt the first explosion of ether behind my eyes that presaged my orgasm. Then it was on me, like a wave, creeping up the startled hairs on my arms and legs and smashing its way out of me. I started to come in spurts that crossed the distance between us, splattering the back of Grove's thighs, calves, and heels. I let out a long sighing groan, and the ether behind my eyes engulfed me for an instant sending everything else into a flash of blackness.

And then it was over, and Grove was up and laughing and toweling himself off. And I smeared his come across my chest and stomach and let it dry there as we stood naked on the balcony, watching the stars, and finishing off the lukewarm coffee. I watched Grove's animated smile as he talked about the stars and the dark outline of the Mexican shoreline in the near distance, and I knew that somehow, despite his clear design, despite his careful construction of the demarcations, we had somehow stepped across the line.

And so he was married to Lucy and I toasted the happy couple at their reception and I slept alone the next night, curled around a pillow stuffed with feathers and memories. And the next night I slept with a performer from one of the lounge acts, missing breakfast and lunch and finally, that evening in Mazatlan, missing the boat altogether.

And now, a decade later, I still feel the sting of loss and the menace of boundaries and the sadness of empty train platforms holding me rigidly to my seat, despite the fact that the man with whom I share this lonely compartment is toying playfully with his long, thin cock, eyeing me speculatively and licking his lips. I watch this moment unfold before me in the flickering cinematic images that play in the blank spaces behind my eyes. *I am a camera*, I think as I begin to record the moment, not on the permanent stock where Grove resides, but on a tape whose quality is marginal, whose images dance with the static of disconnection and shimmer slightly, making it difficult to see the lines that divide individuals. Is that mine? Is that his? Is that me? Is that him? Do I care?

I unbutton my jeans, unzip my zipper, and pull my hard cock out of my jeans. I watch the smile spread across his thin lips. "*Nicht berühren*," I whisper, *Don't touch*. I glance at my reflection in the window then look back at this stranger as he kneels on the floor in front of me.

MASS ASS

Robert Patrick

A boy at the baths
Opened legs thin as laths
    To invite any dick up his ass.
We clustered to fuck
This divine piece of luck,
    Ev'ry putz in the place hard as glass.

We had come off the streets
Hunting fuckable seats
    Scorning bars and the park's grubby groves,
Seeking nooky, not names
Or good spirits or games
    Where hot crotches abounded in droves.

The baths was alive
As if drones in a hive
    Had come crawling for all they could get.

We crowded the halls
With a buzz in our balls,
    But no honey was coming as yet.

We dropped down to see
That the steam room was free.
    There was no ass to catch unawares,
And none in the cool,
Under-used swimming pool.
    We returned to the hall-hell upstairs.

There were pungent perfumes
From occasional rooms
    But most doors were annoyingly shut
As their renters, like me,
Walked around cockily,
    Rather randomly roaming in rut.

Every man there possessed
What the others liked best,
    Whether asshole or hard-on or mouth,
But it looked like the nest
Never would come to rest,
    And all hopes of connections went south.

Though the usual thing
At the baths was to fling
    Your door open and get yourself some,
On a night like tonight
Everyone was uptight
    And nobody was likely to cum.

Every mind in the dim,
Dreamy den was a-brim
    With idyllic, ideal, unreal acts,
Which seemed to eclipse
Any real lips or hips
    Ever coming to grips with bare facts.

So the corridors sludged
As we judged as we trudged
    All around in the shadows in hordes,
And the testicles hung
In between our legs swung
    Full of seed as a garden of gourds.

When the cute youth came in
Through the masses of men,
    He was hot, clearly not there to swim,
For he stripped like a whore
In his wide-open door,
    And we all caught the heat off of him.

To conceal our rude dowels,
We were wrapped in white towels
    But the kid spread his out on his cot,
Then reclined on his back,
Plucked open his crack
    And inserted K-Y up his twat.

Just a blond, bonny boy,
Not in any way coy,
    Undulating gyrating crevasse,

Legs divided and bent
For to better present
    Frontally, cuntily, ass.

The towel was to catch
Any leaks from his snatch,
    All ejaculatory excess.
The thought of those drops
Seeping out of his chops
    Escalated the hall's horniness.

Then the kid closed his eyes,
Elevated his thighs,
    And commanded all cocks in to cum.
Elders bruited around,
"There's a butt wanting browned.
    Better get into line and get some."

Everybody had tongues.
Everybody had bungs.
    Everybody bore seminal pods.
But the catamite's blunt
Self-reduction to cunt
    Ratified ev'rybody as rods.

So I felt myself swell
And I said, "What the hell,"
    And got into the queue to give juice.
I stood with my hand
Underneath my towel, and
    Pulled my pud to be ready for use.

Soon a long line had formed
And we heard the kid stormed
    By the first fuck to enter his door.
How he moaned as the first
Of our company burst
    In his lubricious tube like a boar.

Now the atmosphere was
Brash and bawdy, a-buzz
    With the promise of pending release.
We were boys in a frat
Lucking out, looking at
    A communal, anonymous piece.

We were sailors in port,
Self-advancers at court,
    Soldiers eyeing a drunk in a bunk,
Groaning drones servicing
A great, glistening queen
    Amid sexual, insectual funk.

The kid was reduced
To a gap to get goosed
    By our prods with explosive intent.
As our chargers got charged
His behind was enlarged
    In our minds to a meat monument.

Race, religion, and class
Were dispelled by that ass
    With its massive and passive reproof

That, divested of duds,
We were all silly studs,
    Dumb containers for cum on the hoof.

Men who hardly would greet
If they passed on the street
    In divisive, diverse uniforms
Here were stripped of disguise,
Bound as bulls by the rise
    Of identical sensual storms.

In the backs of our brains
We discovered remains
    Of religions remote as we played
In a crude, incondite
Eleusinian rite
    That was once dignified and arrayed.

We were in Babylon,
Devotees duly drawn
    Toward rolling, controlling white buns
Of a sexual slave
Cleft to show his dark cave
    Where initiates got off their guns.

Deep in wells dug in rocks,
Persians cut off their cocks
    And their balls to become temple whores.
So the boy in the room
Had become a huge womb
    To seduce and reduce our gorged gores.

When such rites were proscribed,
Men were bullied and bribed
    To enact them, defying the state.
In a dark alley-way,
An asshole in Pompeii
    Scrawled the ritual *Show hard, make date.*

This religion, repressed,
Recrudesced and tumesced
    Any time that men gathered with men,
And in barracks and ships
The hot hole in the hips
    Was enjoyed as it always had been.

In Athenian heights
On particular nights
    Men would drink not to think as they sprawled,
Then dishevel their robes
To reveal hairy globes
    With a butthole that begged to be balled.

In Catullus's Rome
With the Capitol's dome
    Hanging, clanging that butt was a vice,
Men ate asses in baths,
Flouting all aftermaths
    Just to service each other's sweet splice.

After pagan defeats,
In monastic retreats
    Any pretty young novice was told

That he must grow a beard,
For the Fatherhood feared
    That a fair face would get his ass poled.

In my southwestern land
Where the butthole was banned
    As a joke not to be spoken of,
Cowboys wooed with the song,
"Nights are long, oh, so long.
    Gotta get me somebody to love."

All of us in that line
To defile the divine
    Waiting wound that we heard being had
Had been taught we'd be burned
In hot Hell if we yearned
    To deliver a load in a lad.

But the fever of youth
Told the tenderer truth
    That the cock had to cum in the crack,
So despite gods and laws
We were lined up because
    Gut was good and we wouldn't turn back.

As engorgement peeled husks
Off the tips of our tusks,
    Our sarongs bulged with prongs like pale fruits.
We all jerked uncontrolled
Through the waistband or fold
    Of the towels that enshrouded our shoots.

We wankers in line,
Feeling phallic and fine,
    Gaily joked as we stroked our taut tools.
Buggers worshiping butt,
Shuffling stallions in rut,
    We all broke one of Everard's rules

As we tugged off our towels
Among manly avowals
    That the damned things were feeling too tight.
Uncontained cocks and balls
Sent their scents down the halls
    As we waited for nooky that night.

All the bored employees.
Police-force retirees,
    Saw us standing illicitly stripped
And were moved to object,
But retired from respect
    Of the god by whom all goads were gripped.

A drunk coming in,
Gaped to see naked men
    As he clawed with a key at his door,
And a dick brushed my butt
And my prick pushed a rut
    As we jostled toward our hot whore.

For, oh, what a mass
Of assailable ass
    Hung available there where we stood.

And oh, what a stock
Of respectable cock,
    And we wondered if maybe we should...

So we played as we pleased
With the asses we squeezed
    And the cocks that we teased in the gloom,
But we all knew we must
Hold our trophies in trust
    For the priestess oiled up in her room.

The drunk stumbled out,
Waving hard-on about,
    Looking funky and phallic and fine,
Then staggered to stand
Towel and tool in each hand
    At the end of the lumbering line.

Like great droplets of dew
Or thick globules of goo,
    Devotees shuffled forward like slaves
As the pricks who had spilled
Came out limp and fulfilled
    Like the undead released from their graves.

When a man entered in
To that vaginal den,
    Every aching erection would pulse,
Throbbing just on the verge
Of a seminal purge
    As we heard each hot cocksman convulse.

Every brain in the chain
Fucked again and again
    That vicarious, visualized slit.
Every act grew more quick
As each man felt his prick
    Growing closer and closer to it.

How I swallowed a laugh,
Stimulating my staff
    While forbidding my seed to disperse
In the glory and grief
Of suspended relief
    Not unlike certain techniques of verse.

Then a fucker came out
Drooling cum from his spout,
    And the cock before mine climbed the kid.
I ogled the mass
Of his big apple-ass
    Slapping happily as he slip-slid.

My genitals got
So unbearably hot
    That I let my hand slide to the tip,
For had I clutched the rod
I'd have shot out my wad
    Watching that big behind grind and grip.

I felt what he felt
As he made his dick melt
    In the ass that already was soaked,

And I wanted my stump
In his high-riding rump
 Which made mean little mouths as he poked.

I was wildly aroused
By the thought of what housed
 His exploring and goring extreme,
And I'd seen the huge knob
On his fat little lob,
 Just the thing to give gut a good ream,

And his heaving, hot hole
Writhing out of control
 Made my schlong long to ruin his rear,
And panting to pole
Someone in the male role
 Had me feeling incredibly queer.

I twiddled my glans
And the next willing man's,
 While I watched all I saw of the fun:
Just my forefucker's seat
And a pair of pale feet
 On his shoulders as he got his gun.

My pulse muttered, "I
Could cram into that guy
 To fuck him as he bucks in that bung,
And the next guy, you see,
Could get on and in me—"
 But I just squeezed my meat where it hung.

Never, ever before,
As I eyed his back door,
    Had I so longed to stuff a butt's yawn.
I was me, I was him,
We were us, we were them
    Who'd observe us in rut and climb on.

Universally male,
Universally hale,
    Universally under cock's curse,
Universally rapt,
Universally trapped,
    Yawning yoni was our universe.

So I watched my prior priest
In the butt of the beast,
    The upreared reliquary he raunched,
His desirable duff
Undulating to stuff
    Where so many lewd loads had been launched.

I was flexing my thighs.
There were tears in my eyes
    And my lips were parched dry from hot breath.
My pelvis was just
An amalgam of lust
    As he labored for his little death.

Then, when he'd gotten off,
He got off with a cough
    And came out with a whispered, "Hot shit."

Then my shadow obscured
The asshole that allured
    As I felt for, then fell into it.

Oh, the state of that hole
As I put in my pole!
    It was drippily, slippily wet,
More a sluice than a slice,
Or, to be more concise,
    As appealing as asshole can get.

For the thought of the cocks
That had shot molten rocks
    Up that gully that so fully gaped,
And their bouncing behinds
As they blew out their minds,
    Made it their poles and assholes I raped.

My vagina on view
As I fucked the foul flue,
    My buns billowing open and shut,
I muscled him mean,
For I envied that queen
    All the men who had been up his butt.

I was wholly aware
Of my hole in the air
    As I fucked in his slushy, hot mush,
And my knowing the next
Dick desired what I flexed
    Made me pop in that slop with a gush.

Then I sighed and half-swooned
And withdrew from the wound,
    Shoving by the next guy in the chain,
Grunting, "Fucking great gash,"
As I stalked off to splash
    In the shower and piss down the drain.

As I strolled the cell-block,
Looking now for rock cock,
    There were plenty of men still lined up
With their towels on their necks,
Salivating for sex
    Mad to add to the cum in the cup.

It was just a dark cell,
Not the heavenly hell
    Where I'd just been the man of all men.
But the line, it would seem,
Was still dreaming that dream,
    And the drunk guy was just going in.

They were zombies in thrall
To a mystical call
    Which no longer now beat in my bone,
And their queen a mere pawn
As I passed them by, drawn
    By a mystical call of my own.

I located by smell
A pitch-black orgy-cell,
    Where on hard cement platforms and shelves

Men beyond or above
Holding out for true love
    Polymorphously proffered themselves.

There I felt lots of rungs
And I smelt lots of bungs,
    Then I fell down ass-up on the floor
To get fucked by a crew
Of butt-fuckers whose goo
    I'd been fucking in minutes before.

THE DOCTOR IS IN

Daniel W. Kelly

My specialty of medical practice isn't the most glamorous, and it's usually the butt of jokes. Like that one, for example. But my personal favorite is *What's it like working with a bunch of assholes every day?*

The thing is, once in a while, an asshole really stands out in a crowd—or should I say, a crack. And this particular time, the asshole belonged to a patient named Ron. The first time Ron came in, it was because his primary care physician had suggested he start going yearly for a thorough prostate exam and all that en-"tails," since he was reaching the ripe young age of thirty-five.

The instant I saw Ron, I had one of those fleeting moments where I felt like my profession was well worth all its downsides

—or backsides, in this case.

Sorry. Those bad puns start to rub off on me, so I try to beat others to the punch.

Anyway, before I'd even stepped into the examination room, my assistant, Steve, a young, hunky nurse whom I hired as much for his appearance as for his resume, handed me the paperwork on a clipboard and whispered, "Something scrumptious waiting in room three for ya."

Steve really knew how to call them. He'd had my patient strip down to his underwear and socks—that's procedure, honest. I was presented with a stocky, hairy man, sitting with legs apart, and doing a hell of a job of filling the crotch of his gray boxer-briefs. Occasionally, a guy really packs a bulge with what are obviously larger than average testicles and penis. Ron was one of those guys. He had muscular hairy thighs and calves, and his stomach was pretty flat, his chest full, and his arms, which were pushing down on each side of the examination table he was sitting on, revealed well-defined triceps.

When he looked up at me, I could have melted. His head was shaven and showed a thin layer of stubble—his brazen way to combat a receding hairline. His chiseled features were sculpted by a few days' worth of whiskers. He had a really sexy, slightly crooked and swollen boxer's nose and gorgeous sky blue eyes. Of course, I couldn't help but notice the wedding ring on his finger.

I had him describe his overall health in what turned out to be a strong but subdued baritone. I asked how his digestive system was doing as a whole, and he said it was good, that he made sure to eat fiber and followed a nutritious diet and exercise regime. I told him in a very professional, doctor-to-patient tone that I could see that he stayed fit.

Then it was time for the general exam. I plugged my stetho-scope into my ears and placed the other end on his swollen pec. His soft chest hair tickled my hand as I listened to his heart, and I watched one of his ample nipples turn hard as a reaction to the cold metal instrument. I moved near the other nipple to even things out, and unable to control myself, allowed the tips of my fingers to accidentally brush over the nipple. It, too, turned hard.

My heart was beating double the time of Ron's, and I reminded myself that this was a patient. I finished the general exam, then explained how exactly the prostate exam was given. While turning to the supply cabinet, I asked him to drop his underwear and bend over on top of the exam table.

I slipped on a white rubber glove (resisting the urge to give the wristband an ominous sounding snap), grabbed a tube of lubricant, and turned to Ron.

I nearly popped out of my professionally-pressed pants. Instead of just bending over the top of the table, Ron had climbed onto it, and was now on all fours, his boxer-briefs down to his knees, his family jewels swaying between his legs under a muscular, large, hair-coated ass. It was one of those visions like something out of a Titan porn DVD, rather than the sterile start of a medical exam. I couldn't bring myself to clarify how I'd actually meant for him to position himself, for several reasons. First, I didn't want to embarrass him. Second, as a gay man, I knew that, realistically, the position he was in was a lot more accommodating for what I was about to do than the standard over-the-table or on-the-table-on-the-side positions usually suggested to protect patient modesty. And third, it just looked so damn good, and I felt I deserved a little bonus for all my dirty work—that would be the past three over-sixty wrinkly-assed patients, one of whom was a woman.

I had to draw my eyes away from the large-as-promised, incredibly hairy package dangling between those thunder thighs, and focus on the equally bushy butt above. I explained to Ron that he would feel coldness and then something that might be a bit uncomfortable. I squirted a glob of lube on my index finger, and and then used it and the thumb on my other hand to separate the forest between his asscheeks to find his anus.

It was one healthy anus: gorgeous, breathtaking, a work of art. The surrounding skin was a deep pink-purple. But his anus was definitely not that of a gay man. It was a nearly invisible hairline crack. It was only when I painted it with a finger of lube that it sunk inward from the chill and showed what it might be capable of swallowing. I heard a hushed intake of air from Ron at the touch of the lube, and noticed his testicles—which were nearly as big as tennis balls and ten times as fuzzy—tighten up below my hand.

I slid my index finger gently but steadily into his grip. When it popped through the initial tight ring of his bunghole, I felt around his quite healthy rectum and checked out his prostate. And once again, I could hear Ron's low *I'm taking it like a man* grunt, more often heard in some teeth-gritting frat initiation. It so fucking turned me on I felt like probing him a bit longer than I would the usual patient. But I didn't. I had ethics. And my professional touch had no real reason to be in there any longer.

As I rolled off the glove and tossed it in the trash, I told him he could pull his underwear back up. Anxious inside at the thought of missing my one opportunity, I turned to

casually look at him as he did so. He was sort of simultane-
ously pulling up his boxer-briefs while getting off the table,
and I caught a quick glimpse of his ridiculously large cock,
which was at a partially erect stage. It's not unusual for some
men to become aroused from this examination, but most often,
it's my gay patients. I looked quickly away so he wouldn't be
embarrassed, though he didn't seem all that self-conscious. Of
course, if I were that well hung, not much would embarrass
me either.

I gave Ron a clean bill of health and told him to come again
in a year.

And when that year arrived, I was thrilled to find that he was
my last patient of the day. When I walked into the examination room...well, you know how time fades your memory of
someone you've seen only once, and you start to think your
recollection is making him better than he actually was so you
can use that new composite image to masturbate? My memory
couldn't have prepared me for the reality. He had grown a
tough-looking salt 'n' pepper goatee, and this time around, his
boxer-briefs were dark blue. I gave him the usual knee-weak-
ening physical checkup (his nipples were more delectable than
before), but before I could tell him to drop his underwear for
me, he said he knew the drill, and once again climbed his hot
ass up on the exam table.

I slipped on the old glove (okay, a new, sanitary glove) and
grabbed the lube. He was definitely looking like an old pro
who knew the drill was coming. He had his back well arched,
so his cheeks were widely spread, and I could almost make out
his deep purple anus through his crack hair. His big balls and
dick were even more prominently dangling between his legs

than the year before, and his friggin' dick had already become semierect. I really fought a losing battle to keep my own dick from being in the same state in my pants. Hopefully, I would be able to control it before it grew past half-mast.

This time around, when I'd parted the cheeks completely and tickled his anus with a finger stroke of the gel, it pulsed harder than the previous year, and his groan was a lot louder. This guy was turning me on so bad, I had to keep reminding myself it was business, not pleasure—although it really pleased me to finger his ass. I felt around a bit, and once again, he took it like a—gutturally groaning—man. I explained that I just wanted to do a slightly more thorough rectal. I applied more lube to both my index finger and my middle finger. I warned him that this was going to feel more intense. And boy, did it. He gripped me like a Venus flytrap. His groan sounded almost sexual, rising in pitch as my combined fingers buried themselves inside him.

Just at that moment there was a light knock on the door, and Steve poked his head in to tell me the test results were in for one of my patients, and that I should look at them before I left for the night. Fact was, Steve had already told me that *before* I came in to see Ron, and I knew damn well he just wanted to get a peek at the patient we both had a crush on. While he was giving me this recycled information, I worked on Ron's insides without focusing much, so I was sort of wiggling my fingers around inside of him with no real motive—or no *good* motive.

Steve always looks adorable in his snug male nurse uniform, and his masculine presence is strongly felt when he's in a room, so he apologized for intruding and called over Ron's shoulder for him to not be modest because Steve saw this kind of thing all day long and didn't think twice about it. Then he looked at me and let his eyes pulse wide while mouthing the word *HOTTT!*

As soon as Steve was gone, I turned my focus back to Ron's domes, and began to dig inside him again, when I felt his asshole convulsing, making mincemeat out of my fingers. Ron suddenly grunted, "Shit!" and next thing I knew cum was flying out of his now fully erect monster cock, soaking the blue boxer-briefs bundled under his knees. There was nothing I could do. My fingers were at his mercy. I had to wait until his climax was complete before his strangling sphincter finally released them.

I immediately withdrew them as he turned over. I don't know which one of us had a redder face. He was speechless while I grabbed disposable towels nervously from the supply cabinet for him to clean up with, explaining that it was okay, nothing to be embarrassed by, that it happened sometimes, that the male G-spot was located in the rectum, and some men who didn't even know it have extremely sensitive G-spots. He murmured, "Okay" as he wiped cum from his thighs and his boxer-briefs, then stood and wiped globs of lubricant from his asscrack before shamefacedly pulling up his undies. I took the balled-up towels from him with my gloved hand and tossed them. Then I exited, giving him a chance to dress in private.

I *also* needed privacy. I locked myself in my office, heart thudding against my chest. I was imagining Ron getting all homophobic about his reaction to a prostate exam and accusing me of sexual harassment. I could be slapped with a huge lawsuit—have my license taken away. I was absolutely terrified.

And that terror stayed with me for exactly two weeks.

"One more patient to go, and we're outta here," Steve said as he handed me a clipboard, his daily last-call routine.

He didn't move as I looked at the paperwork in my hand. I saw why.

"Is this right?" I asked, confused.

"Yep. After his last checkup, he told me he needed to schedule a follow-up appointment with you in two weeks—and he specifically asked for the final appointment of the day again," Steve explained.

"Wait a minute. He asked for the final appointment last year, too?" I asked, and Steve responded with one raised eyebrow and a nod. "What's this about?"

"I could guess." Steve flashed his charming smile and winked. "Nervous?"

"Just don't go too far away," I requested. Damn right I was nervous.

"Got it, boss," Steve replied. I love when he calls me that—especially during sex—but that's another erotic story.

I took a deep breath and approached the door. I pushed it open—and it seemed all my blood was rushing to my dick, leaving my face ghostly pale.

God, he looked good. He was in tightly clinging black boxer-briefs. I wondered if he consciously remembered what color he wore at each appointment so as not to repeat. His broad back faced me as he stood on the exam room scale, fiddling with the mechanisms. His ass muscles strained against the material of his underwear.

"Hey, doc," he said as I shut the door. "I can't seem to get a good reading on this thing."

I walked over with a totally put-on, professional demeanor, and from behind him, I adjusted the sliding weights until a healthy two-hundred seventeen balanced things out. I was so close to him I could breathe in the scent of his soap, his shampoo, and its gentle blend with the perspiration released since his shower. It was like sleeping gas. I wanted to close my eyes and dream happy thoughts.

"So, why back so soon? Everything okay?" I asked, still standing behind him. He finally turned and looked at me. And pointed at me accusingly—with a swollen arrow-straight cock nearly puncturing his tight boxer-briefs, making them even tighter in the process. I looked at it in appreciative awe.

His face and bald head had turned a heated red. "I think I need you to examine me again. More thoroughly than last time." He looked me sternly straight in the eyes, making it clear that he was still a man, in control of the situation.

"Okay." I nodded, staring back into his sky blue eyes. It was an odd sort of standoff, neither of us willing to appear like we wanted this more than the other.

I grabbed the end of my stethoscope and placed it over one of his swelling nipples, chilling it into a nugget to nibble on. He sighed and shivered, as if he'd walked into a meat freezer. I could practically see mist spilling from his luscious lips. I could *actually* hear his heartbeat, and it was as dangerously over the speed limit as mine this time.

I moved to the other side, to make the pair of nipples twins again. His powerful legs threatened to give out, and he fell slightly backward, clawing for the scale to steady himself. Once he'd finished with his balancing act, and I'd finished giving his other nipple equal time, I let the stethoscope fall back against my torso.

He stood without dropping his gaze. I reached authoritatively for the lube and glove, and you damn well better believe there was an ominous pornlike wristband snap this time.

"I need you to drop your underwear and get up on the table," I directed. He did as told. "Lower your face all the way down to the table. Right. Stay like that. I'll be with you in one second." I was taking command.

His hairy cheeks split open, his oversized genitals filled the space between his thighs, and his cockhead dragged the tabletop. I watched him closely as I moved to a nearby intercom unit.

"Steven?"

"Yeah. I'm here, boss."

"I'm going to need your assistance," I said, and then let go of the intercom button without waiting for a reply.

Ron didn't flinch—or protest.

I was too nervous to do this alone, I knew Steve wouldn't forgive me if I didn't include him (he and I had played doctor together in this very room after office hours numerous times), and I knew Ron wasn't looking for a relationship with me. He was definitely just here to have me do a job either his wife never would, or one he was just too much of a man to ask her to do.

I picked up another disposable glove, and when Steve walked in, I tossed it at him. He's athletic, and has good reflexes. He caught it immediately, assessed the situation— and the monster cock dangling between our patient's legs— and pulled on the glove without question. We approached our specimen of man ass.

"I'm going to need you to hold him open while I perform this exam," I instructed.

As Steve gladly gripped both cheeks and yanked them farther apart, both he and I couldn't help but notice the long, glistening stream of precum spilling from Ron's dick. Steve gave me one of his adorable smirks.

My first instinct at seeing Ron's purple pucker fully exposed was to dive right in with my tongue. But that wouldn't be good for my practice—yet. So I lubed up my finger like a professional, and this time, I used the gloved tip to tickle the perimeter of Ron's asshole. He moaned without restraint as his pucker sucked in like a Hoover. I kept circling, gradually putting more pressure against the flesh and spinning in toward his still-tight slit. He slowly began to draw in my whole finger, while I kept up the circular rotation, stretching the walls of his rectum. His beefy body responded. His buttcheeks started to wiggle, which caused his fuck hole to squeeze my finger.

"I think I might need a second opinion," I said to Steve. "Tell me if this feels okay to you."

I took my side of Ron's ass with my free hand, holding his cheek in place while Steve took his now free hand and slowly slid his gloved index finger into Ron, snuggling up against my still inserted finger.

"Oh, geeez!" Ron huffed, still spilling precum. He was most likely going to be leaving the office commando, considering the mess he was making of the boxer-briefs stretched from knee to knee.

I locked eyes with Steve, and we gave each other the visual go-ahead. I pulled out first, all the way, and Ron's purple pucker morphed around Steve's gloved finger, his ass hairs and Steve's glove both glistening with lube. Then Steve slowly exited, and just as Ron's anus tried to seal back up, I weaseled my way back in. We picked up the pace, one finger alternating with the other. Ron's powerful arms clutched the sides of the table, and one side of his face was now pressed firmly against the top of the exam table. His eyes were rolling, and he was breathing so heavily that spit was bubbling between his lips. A low, consistent hum emanated from his larynx.

I reached out with my free hand to undo Steve's pants, releasing his bulge, and he did the same for me. Neither of us stopped plunging our fingers up Ron's hairy hole, though. Once we were both swinging free, I snatched up the tube of lubricant and squeezed a line across the top of Steve's cock, following his vein for guidance, then did the same to my own cock. I also squeezed a glob between our fingers as they worked Ron's pucker. This was all about multitasking. I moved closer to Steve, and smeared both of our cocks with the lube, wrapped my hand around both at the same time so they were trapped together within my fist, and began stroking slowly. Steve's upper body relaxed at the sensation.

I looked to Ron's hairy moon to show Steve that it was time to up the ante. On my next journey into Ron's fuck tunnel, my middle finger joined my index finger. Ron cried out—bordering on a squeal—as the two fingers went back in, followed by Steve's two fingers. We showed no mercy. We scooped our way around his rectum, yanking his sphincter walls in all directions.

It was an out-of-body experience—I was visualizing my assistant and myself from across the room, our pants down, our cocks conjoined, our fingers jammed up my gorgeous patient's ass. This was so wrong, but there was no room for rationality. This was all about selfish satisfaction, about the world feeling good. There were no consequences.

And Ron would completely agree with me. We'd taken him to new levels of ecstasy. He was whimpering like a puppy. I couldn't see his face, but I had no doubt that euphoric tears were pooling in his eyes—and that his body had turned to mush as he gave up completely to the sensation.

Steve blew first. I felt his manhood throb between my palm

and cock, and then his hot cum splattered into my pubic hairs and onto my shaft as I continued to stroke both of us.

As much as I wanted this feeling to go on forever, I wanted the release more. I continued to work my cock as Steve's dropped out of the picture—and my palm. I curled the two fingers I had in Ron's ass downward and poked away with a frenzy at his prostate. Steve joined me.

The response was immediate and violent. Ron's entire body clenched, his powerhouse stomach muscles tightening and pulling him into a fetal position. It felt, from my point of view, like he was about to snap our fingers off with his sphincter. And his near-soprano shriek practically blew out my eardrum. I was helpless to assist with steadying him because my load was now set in motion. All I could do was watch as I sprayed onto the exam room floor.

Steve was forced to jump to Ron's aid, cradling the large man in his strong arms—one of which was still reaching back to Ron's ass, where Steve's fingers were still stuck—and embracing him so he wouldn't fall off the table. Ron's body fell heavily onto Steve's torso, but Steve was more than able to hold him in place. Ron's cum sprayed from his huge erection with no rhyme or reason, arcing out of sight as it hit every object in the vicinity.

As his convulsing slowed, we felt his sphincter loosen its hold a bit and our fingers popped free, which resulted in another shock to Ron's system. Steve helped him roll onto his back, and he lay there, his bearish chest heaving. His face was flushed, and his bald head gleamed with sweat. His eyes were closed as he focused on regaining his breath, strength, and equilibrium.

"Relax, big fella," Steve said, rubbing Ron's shoulder.

Steve has a great voice for soothing nervous patients. It's so calming...and fucking sexy.

Now that I'd ejaculated, logic flooded back, and I had to step away from the scenario. I cleaned myself off with a disposable towel, tossed the glove, and dressed my bottom half quickly. Then I turned to Steve, who stood patiently beside our patient, and said, "Can you handle it from here?"

Steve nodded, I thanked him, and once again, I allowed a run-in with Ron to banish me to my office. I just didn't know how to interact with the man after something like that. What to do, what to say.

And I have no idea what Steve said to him either, but before leaving the office, Ron scheduled an appointment for the following month—the final appointment of the day.

So yeah, maybe I do work with a bunch of assholes all day... but, once in a while, the only way to deal with an asshole is to be a real jerk-off.

MR. LAUNDRY

Lee Houck

While I'm standing at the window, he appears.

Every Friday night the heavy door swings open and Mr. Laundry carries his dirty clothes to the Laundromat. He drags the army green bag down the stairway and then, with one thick heave, using his shoulder like a crowbar, he brings the load to rest behind his head, arms stretching out to the edges of the bag. Tonight he's wearing a red T-shirt with the sleeves torn off (I can see a tattoo on his right arm), worn jeans, and frumpy tennis shoes. I want to rake my hands underneath his shirt, feel the soft warm fibers against the tough tight sinew of his body. Snake my mouth along the textures of his chest—smooth and hard near his shoulder, mushy padded sweaty near his armpit, the relaxed weight of his pectoral, the delicate change of flesh around his nipple, sensitive and flooded with blood. Slowness, gentleness, pours out of every pore of his body. I wonder if this is who he is.

I've been watching him for two months.

I gather my clothes, dividing items that can wait another week from the worst-smelling stuff, which I wad down into a drawstring sack. I scrounge quarters from the change jar, walk down the stairs and out onto the sidewalk.

When I get to the Laundromat, a short Mexican woman is washing the tops of the machines with a rag and talking on the phone. She's chatting with whoever about whatever in a language that's all vowels, lugging a heavy cart of wet clothes behind her, rolling it through the aisles. Mr. Laundry is here, and he isn't supposed to be. It's Tuesday—not his day. His eyes follow me as I walk around the other side of the folding table. Part of me wants this to happen. Part of me is really horny. Part of me can't speak.

He walks right up to me. "Can I borrow some soap?"

I know I've got a script somewhere for this kind of thing. How many times have I drummed up stupid conversation? But this is something different, and I'm nervous.

He repeats himself. "Soap. Can I borrow some?" He tugs at his shirttail.

"I don't bring it with me." Brilliant answer. What are you, a genius?

He leans against the vibrating machine, arms folded across his chest, his feet crossed at the ankle. Seeing him up close, the details appear: jeans worn at the cuffs, left leg more frayed than the right, skin wrinkled in the crook of his elbow, the tattoo on his arm, a lot of hair on his knuckles. I don't know what to say. Then I do.

"Here's fifty cents. You can use the vending machine over there." I pull two coins from my pocket and stretch my arm out to him. He pauses, stands up straight, and walks over to me. He lifts his hand up and everything zooms in on this tiny moment, the part where my fingers drop the coins into his rough dark palm. The world slows.

"Thanks," he says, smirking, charming.

"Sure."

"Slow morning."

"Yeah." I notice my arm is still hanging out in the open.

"So you live around here?"

It's an odd question to ask at a Laundromat, I think—is this supposed to be his pickup line? "Yeah, right across the street."

"You like it?"

"I love it."

"I've been here almost a year," he says. "I see the same people walking around, same people coming home from work every day. Same people going to work every day."

"You start to recognize them and then you wonder if anyone starts to recognize you." We pause. He smacks his gum. I see his clean white teeth.

"So what do you do?"

"You mean for a living?"

"Yes."

I look over my shoulder for a hint of how to answer his question. None comes. So I concentrate hard, pushing all the synapses in my brain to work together. Pushing toward a synchronized electronic buzz. I count to four. Like a brown blanket tossed over a fire, the world becomes flat. The air smells like ashes, molten marshmallow cinders.

"I'm a hustler," I say.

"You're kidding," he says.

"No." The flat place is wide and blank, and you can see for miles if you want to.

Mr. Laundry leans in close and whispers to me. "Can I ask you something?" I can smell the mint on his breath. The same Doublemint gum that my grandparents gave me in church, to make me stop squirming.

"Sure."

"How much for the whole night?"

The parade of spinning clothes pulsates behind him in a long syncopated line. I look closer at the squareness of his jaw and the stubble along his neckline. I want to touch his lips with mine, taste his tongue, smell him tomorrow on my fingers. "What do you want?" I ask.

"I've got five hundred in cash at the apartment. I'll get you more if you want it."

"My clothes," I say. He pulls some money from his back pocket and walks it over to the attendant. He talks to her in Spanish. "What did you tell her?" I ask when he returns.

"She's going to fold them and you can pick them up tomorrow."

"What a gentleman," I say.

"I do what I can."

"Do you speak Spanish?"

"A little." He opens the door and the cold air from outside collides with the warm air from the dryers, blowing around the runty dust bunny tornadoes.

"You're not a serial killer are you?"

"I don't think so," he says.

"You'll have to excuse him, he always does that." The dog, furry, brown, and dripping with slobber, nudges his face into my crotch.

"It's okay. I'm used to it."

He grabs the dog by his collar and tries to tug him from between my legs. "He mostly sleeps all day. He's kind of old. Nine. I mean, pretty old for a mastiff." He scratches his shoulder, then his head, scrunching his face like he's thinking hard. I can't wait to get my mouth on that tattoo.

"What's his name?" I say.

"Caleb. It means brave. Or victorious, depending on who you talk to." The dog laps at his face, covering his beard in drool. He smiles and laughs. I'm going to have to kiss the mouth that just kissed Caleb.

"Right."

"It's stupid, I guess."

"No. It's nice. Fitting."

Nervous again, I send myself to the place where everything is flat. Where the senses perk up, the vision clears, and the animal in you can float up to the surface. I'm sort of absently rubbing my dick, habit I guess, but it's not hard yet. I wonder if I'll be able to fuck him. I wonder if he wants me to.

"Yeah," he says. He picks mail off the table, stuffs it under some junk in the kitchen. He snaps a dirty shirt off the back of the chair, like he's trying to impress me, throws it into the bathroom where it falls onto a heap of socks and underwear, a quiet lump. I sit in a big leather armchair and open my legs. The leather feels like safety and goodness.

Caleb jumps into my lap. He weighs a ton. His paws are as big as my hands and drool drips out of his mouth onto my jeans. "I think he needs a bib or something."

"Sorry. Here." He hands me a towel that's only semidry. "You can wipe it up with this." It only spreads the goop around on my pants. "God, I'm sorry."

"Thanks. It's okay."

"You want a drink or something?"

"I don't drink."

"Smoke?"

"Or smoke either."

"Good, I hate cigarettes."

"Then why did you offer me one?"

"I don't know," he says.

"If I had said yes, would you have had a cigarette to offer me?"

"Never mind."

"So what's your name?"

"Aiden. What's yours?"

"Simon."

"Is that your real name?"

"Yes."

Aiden holds a knotted rope down near the dog's mouth, half playing with him, half talking to me, and Caleb slides off my lap. I wonder if he has bought sex before. Maybe.

"Well, I thought you would use a fake name or something."

"No, just Simon."

"I guess not." He counts five hundred dollars in twenties and puts the stack on the table near the kitchen. He turns away from me as he counts.

"This is going to sound weird," he says.

"I've heard it all."

"No, I mean—are there things you won't do?"

"I told you I do everything."

"Because in *Pretty Woman* she wouldn't kiss on the mouth and stuff like that."

I laugh. "No. I'll kiss you on the mouth. That's fine."

"Sorry," he says.

"Stop apologizing." My dick is hard now, but I don't remember it happening.

He kneels. He plays with my dick through my jeans and then unbuttons the fly.

"So, you're not going to beat me up are you?"

"No," he says. "Whatever gave you that idea?"

"You never know."

Next, we're in his bed and I'm naked. He rubs his hand up and down my whole body. I'm thrusting my cock slowly into his mouth while he's got one finger in my ass. He feels like wet velvet. I lay my head back.

The flat place shrinks, pulls away first at the edges, then begins to look a little like this room. The horizon bends to make doorways, and furniture appears. The burning marshmallow stink vanishes, leaving only the clean sheets, the hardwood floor. The change happens so slowly that I don't realize it's changing until it's different, the previous moment gone forever, and then I'm here. Right here with him.

The flat place echoes like a memory, its absence like a sickening déjà vu that amplifies the details, and the curious, gentle minutes spent with Aiden. If I wanted to remember them, could I?

Everything in the world is dissolving.

Aiden has his pants undone. He jerks off and comes while he's sucking me, which isn't rare, really. After he gets his rhythm started up again, sucking harder on the upstroke and letting it slide on the down, I come. He takes his pants off and then the rest of his clothes. He lies down next to me and rubs his hand across my head where I'm sweating.

He closes my eyes with his fingers, then touches them, barely, to my lips. He pulls the sheets and blankets over us. I turn over, onto my stomach, and he reaches his arm around me, runs his thumb up and down my spine.

Things settle and congeal. No noise. Only breathing. And the flat place is another country, inaccessible, a muddy Polaroid of a strange land where you once were.

I turn and press my face into his chest. I nuzzle my nose in the hair between his pecs, inhaling the moistness. I burrow my head under his chin, both palms flat against his chest. I can't get close enough. Aiden bends his head down and kisses my forehead. His fuzzy chin tickles my face.

In the morning I get up and take the money off the table, taking only two hundred and fifty, leaving the rest—feeling sort of bad about overcharging. Aiden is still sleeping, the sheet wrapped low around his waist, his shoulders spread out on the mountain of pillows. I stare down at the tattoo on his arm, a hollow hand, with a wheel of symbols inside—a tiny horse, a star, and a curvy line that looks like a river—bluish-green, smaller than I thought, and oddly soothing. I refill the dog's water dish and let myself out.

GIOVANNI

Logan Zachary

I stood in the doorway, uncertain of where to go
or what to do. Remington's was a male strip club
in Toronto. The sign read COVER CHARGE $5,
but no one was manning the front door. I pulled
out an American five and looked around.

A young man danced on the stage, wearing
only a pair of white briefs and tennis shoes.
The music blared around the semicrowded
room. It was early. I looked to the bartender,
who was busy filling mugs of beer. My glance
returned to the stage, where the lad's briefs
were now down around his ankles. His business stood semierect and danced in time to his
pelvic thrusts.

Arms wrapped around my shoulders and
pulled me close. "Enjoying what you see?" a
young voice asked in my ear.

I turned to see a shirtless man with a smooth, pale chest. His torso looked sculpted from stone. A thin triangle of fine dark hair ran from his belly button and disappeared into his surf shorts. His black hair was cut short and spiked straight up.

My mouth was dry and I couldn't swallow. "I just got here. Where...where do I pay the..." I waved my bill at the sign.

"Forget about that, spend it on what counts." He winked at me. He stepped back so I could get a better look. No fat on this boy. Young and firm. Very nice looking, but not my type; he looked barely nineteen.

Still, my eyes caressed his form before I looked over his shoulder to the stage. The dancer was exhibiting his dick in full glory as the music came to a close.

"Give a hand to Dante. He'll be walking around soon," said an anonymous voice from the speakers. The dancer pulled on his underwear and descended the stairs. He walked to a back hallway and disappeared. "Give it up for Chance," said the voice. A man strolled to the stage wearing a cowboy hat, chaps, and holster. His vest flapped open, showing a six-pack to die for.

"I'm Carlos. I'll be dancing soon." The man next to me guided my attention back to him.

I smiled and nodded.

My confusion must have been easily read, since he continued. "Do you know how this place works?" He took my hand and ran it down his warm chest to where the fine hair began.

This was my first time, I didn't have a clue.

"All the dancers have a set on stage and then they walk and work the floor. We talk to the customers." He ran his fingers through my blond curls and continued. "And if you like what you see, you can have a private dance."

My eyes widened.

"Upstairs." His eyes looked to the back of the bar. "Private rooms, so you can be alone with the dancer, and get a special dance."

I swallowed hard. That wasn't the only thing hard.

"What are you drinking?" he asked.

My mind was spinning. Alcohol was not a good idea. "Just a Coke."

"I'll be right back." He started off and then returned. He took the five from my hand and walked to the bar. Tight shorts hugged his perfect butt.

"Keep the change," I called. At least I hoped there would be change.

A thin blond wearing a wrestler's unitard sauntered toward me, paused, then walked by. An olive-skinned man approached, also paused, looked over my shoulder, and veered to the left.

What was wrong with me? Could they tell I was a tourist? Was I marked by Carlos?

A warm breath blew across the back of my neck. Someone was behind me.

I turned slowly and saw why everyone was making a wide berth. My breath caught in my throat.

My five-year-old nephew collects Rescue Hero figures. I buy them for him for Christmas and his birthday. Here was one of them, live and in the flesh. This was the one I wanted to play with. A pair of Levi's were painted on his perfect body. A thick, black leather belt with two hooks surrounded his narrow waist. He wore black leather boots on his feet and he had no shirt. Thank you.

He walked up to me and smiled. Holding out his hand he said, "I'm Giovanni."

I bet you are, I thought.

His chest hair was cropped short against his tanned chest, an even covering that added contrast to his rippling muscles. His pecs fanned out and sloped to a washboard stomach. His treasure trail made the perfect hourglass pattern. He was— just right, a Rescue Hero come to life.

Carlos returned with my Coke. Giovanni thanked him. He took the glass and handed it to me. Carlos stood for a second, started to glare, but before he could say anything, the announcer called him to the stage. He ran his hand through his spikes and headed away.

My body swooned and I sidestepped to a table nearby. I leaned against it, hoping it would hold me up.

"Enjoying your stay in Toronto?" Giovanni's hand played down my side as he moved next to me. We watched Carlos untie his drawstring. His surf shorts slipped lower. The crests of his butt glowed in the spotlight. My heart quickened.

Giovanni's voice was smooth. "Did he tell you how this works? You pay by the song for the special dances upstairs." I watched as the wrestler guided a man in his sixties to the back hall, then glimpsed Dante, back on the club floor, with the hand of a blond football player tucked into the back of his underwear, both men laughing and whispering.

"So, do you want a dance?" Giovanni's hand stroked my neck and played with my curls .

I couldn't speak. He was perfect, but I wasn't sure what to do.

"You're shy. I think that's cute." He continued to play with my hair and ran a finger down the opening of my shirt. His nail combed through my chest hair. "Is there another dancer you like better?" he asked. He pointed to Carlos. "He's very hot. Tight butt, big cock."

On stage, Carlos's shorts were off and the yellow jockstrap was working its way down his hips. His ass shone in the spotlight.

I wanted to look at Giovanni, but I also wanted to see what was underneath that pouch.

Giovanni laughed as he watched me struggle. "Enjoy him on stage and enjoy me upstairs."

I took a big sip of Coke, and almost choked as Carlos's cock sprang free from the jock. Giovanni slapped me on the back as ten inches waved at me from the stage.

"I need a little more time," I said between coughs.

Giovanni signaled to the bartender and spun his arm in a circle in the air. The bartender—his voice no longer anonymous—picked up the microphone and announced, "The legendary Giovanni is next."

Giovanni turned and kissed me on the forehead. "For luck," he said. He dashed toward the stage, but instead of ascending the stairs that Carlos was descending, he jumped onto it with one graceful leap.

He started to sway with the music. His spine hugged the pole and he swung around and around, but his eyes never left mine.

And my eyes never left his. He was dancing just for me. The crowded room shrank and all the bodies disappeared. It was just the two of us, and the music. Giovanni opened his belt and ran his hands down his chest, across his stomach, and then under the waistband of his jeans.

His belt flapped as he moved his pelvis so it slapped the pole on stage. His hips gyrated to the right and to the left, then he performed low knee bends and squat thrusts, his eyes never leaving mine. How I could make eye contact and still absorb every detail of his dance was beyond me.

In my heart I wanted to see him take off his clothes, but another part of me wanted the dance to last forever. The song ended and another started. The button on his jeans opened and his flat abdomen was exposed. The fan of hair grew darker and thicker. His belt acted like a coiled dick onstage, flopping one way and the other, again slapping the pole.

My body tingled with the electricity in the room. My heart beat in time with the music.

His zipper lowered, the denim giving release to the rigid flesh beneath. His erection rose from the V as his tight jeans worked their way down his legs to reveal a perfect body. My private Hero. He danced and swayed.

My mouth watered. The music rose and he smiled at me. I smiled back. He cocked his head to the side, toward the back hallway and the upstairs rooms. He glowed with pleasure and excitement. *Do you want a private dance?* he asked me from across the room.

Could I be reading his mind? My body swayed with the music. The beat grew and my palms went damp. I wiped them on my legs and smiled.

Come with me, Giovanni called with his silent glance. *Come with me.* He danced and danced. The music climaxed with the last note.

I said aloud, "Yes."

Applause broke the silence as Giovanni pulled up his pants and zipped before the announcer could say a word.

He jumped off the stage and extended his arm in my direction.

I ran to him.

His hand reached for mine as the audience parted. Our fingers wove together as our palms touched. He pulled me to the hallway and up the stairs. The stairs turned at the top, and we entered a hallway lined with doors to dressing rooms. Giovanni grabbed a key, and we entered one. He motioned for me to sit on the bench and he stood with his hips at my eye level.

"What would you like me to do?" he asked, as the Pointer Sisters' "Dare Me" started. He opened his belt and unzipped his fly. He pushed his pants down to the top of his boots and moved closer.

My hands reached around and cupped his ass. His cheeks fit perfectly into my grip. His buns were warm and tight, covered with a fine down that tickled my hands as my fingers massaged the muscle and explored the crease. Despite his workout onstage, his skin was dry and soft. His tan line showed the tight fit of a Speedo. I licked my lips as my hands rounded his hips and my thumbs lifted his balls. They dangled low and heavy, then rose with my thumbs as my fingers combed through his pubic hair. His erection stood straight out, even bigger than it had appeared onstage. Foreskin sheathed the mushroom end and precum glistened on the fold of skin.

I breathed in deeply, his erection bobbing against the tip of my nose. A musky male scent assaulted my nostrils and I felt faint. *I'm dreaming*, I thought, and I didn't want to wake up. My fingers ran up and down the length of his shaft. My cock pressed hard against my Calvin Kleins, tenting my pants. His foreskin pulled back and the head of his cock slipped out, the pearl of precum glistening before it dropped onto my finger. I rubbed it between my fingertips and savored the sensation.

Giovanni moaned as my fingers encircled his girth, pulling the foreskin back and forth, exposing and covering his sensitive glans.

"What would you like?" he breathed. His wet tip brushed my nose, burning it with the sweet smell of cum.

Before I could speak, his hands worked my fly open. He pulled down my Calvins. A huge wet spot soaked the front. He squeezed the cotton between his fingers and then brought them to his mouth. He licked the ooze off and swallowed deeply, delighting in the taste.

His cock lowered toward my mouth and my tongue lapped his precum, which was sweet and salty, and all male.

His hand squeezed more precum from my briefs and he brought his fingers to my mouth. My juices mixed with his. Ambrosia.

"Want to try something I enjoy?" he asked.

I nodded. I was unable to speak.

He pulled his foreskin down and opened the fold wide. He spit into his hand, wet the folds, and rubbed the head of my cut cock with his other hand. Spreading the precum around, he guided my cockhead into the end of his foreskin. His tip hit my tip and the moisture mixed. He pulled the hood over my cock, securing them together in a vacuum. A sucking sound rose from the mix of spit and precum, as dick met dick in the hood of skin.

My hands grabbed onto his ass and pulled him closer and our dicks humped as my hips met his thrusts. *So this is what it feels like to have a foreskin. Wonderful.*

His hand jacked our cocks at the same time, one huge penis shared by two. His sensation was my sensation. Our hips rocked as my hands worked his ass. My fingers were slippery and found his tight sphincter. My index finger circled the ring and probed the deep pucker in the center.

With each circle of my finger, I pressed harder, and Giovanni pressed back. His asshole was a mouth sucking on my finger, drawing it inside as I pushed. Another pelvic thrust and my finger broke through, into the warmth.

Our rhythm quickened.

The foreskin hood formed suction and more precum added to the seal. Giovanni's hand stroked our two-man tube. Eighteen inches of male pleasure spanned us, joined us, became us. Pearls of juice seeped out and lubricated our common shaft. His hand ran down to the hilt of my cock, and back to the hilt of his. He spread more precum with each pass. Our hips rocked back and forth. I fucked his foreskin and it sucked my cock. Tension grew from the base of my penis and pressure built in my balls. My finger sunk deeper and deeper, seeking his prostate, faster, deeper. My finger found the magic spot. An eruption exploded from his cock, engorging the small skin pocket with hot, wet thickness before spraying through the seal of foreskin and coursing down the length of my shaft, soaking my pubic hair.

As the wave hit, my balls released and matched his load. Giovanni's hand never stopped. More cum spilled out and spread across our cocks. My finger continued to stimulate his gland, producing wave after wave. Our climaxes ended at last, and he pulled back. Foreskin suction popped loudly in the small space. We separated, but my cock strained forward for more. Mine didn't want to release his yet.

I sat back, spent. Giovanni struggled to his feet and found his legs were unable to hold him up. He collapsed on the bench next to me. "Wow. That was wild." He ruffled my hair. Our breath returned to normal.

I reached for my wallet. Giovanni held my wrist.

"What?" I asked confused.

"Why don't we settle up at your place? I get off in a few minutes, we could go out for supper and make a night of it."

"I'm staying at a hotel," I said.

"No problem, we can settle up there too."

"My room has a Jacuzzi."

"It may take us all night to square up," Giovanni said as we walked out of the booth.

"I hope so," I said. "I hope so." And it did.

PHYSICAL THERAPY

Jay Neal

Indeed, it can happen just that fast. Without thinking, I stepped out of the shower and strode naked and wet across the floor of the bathroom to fetch a towel. Before I could even register the fleeting sensation of my wet foot starting to slip on the tiles, I found myself flat on my back saying, "Ouch! Ouch! Ouch!" and trying to find a position for my leg that didn't cause intolerable pain.

There followed plenty of tiresome, time-consuming details we needn't go into: dragging myself to the phone, ambulance (cute med tech!), emergency room, X-rays—it is broken!—operating room, anesthesia, surgery, recovery. Undermining my notion that surgeons only take things out, I am now the proud owner of a metal plate in my upper thigh, screwed into the top of my femur, and sure to arouse the interest of security personnel at any airport.

Recovery meant only rare periods of rest in the orthopedic ward between bouts of taking pills, giving blood, talking about bowel movements, and torture delivered at the hands of the Physical Therapy Brigade.

The Brigade arrived on the ward every morning, bright and cheerful and bringing with them a frightening assortment of infernal devices that would shame the Spanish Inquisition. The Brigade claimed they were there to make one feel better, but I knew that they must secretly be after some very important information. If I knew what it was they wanted to know, I'd happily have confessed.

Every day seemed to bring someone new, undoubtedly because most patients quickly developed a love-hate—mostly hate—relationship with any individual therapist. So far I had myself experienced: 1) the petite, blonde, fairy princess with the relentless sadistic streak; 2) the Wagnerian Brunhild type who seemed dedicated to my personal immolation; 3) the beautiful and unexpectedly strong man from Nigeria whose command of English was perfect except when it came to the vocabulary of pain and words like *stop!*; and 4) the comedy trio I thought of as the Marx Sisters. What—or whom—I wondered, might be on the program for this, my fifth day of so-called recovery following surgery?

The Brigade arrived right on schedule for morning maneuvers, marching through the hall in precision formation, their tools of torture swinging and clanking as they went. We had made it through a weekend of second-string tactical units, so there we were at the top of the week with the A-Team in full force and ready for new challenges. That meant new faces and an excuse for a new burst of optimism on my part, foolish though it may have been, that perhaps I would be visited by a compassionate human being for a change. Ridiculous, naive, and unlikely, I admit, but one must hope: it speeds patient recovery and all that therapeutic jazz.

My optimism was further stirred to see that the Brigade that day included in its ranks someone who was actually cute. Tall, youngish, just chunky enough to verge on husky, with a nice smile, a cheerful face, a spot of red coloring on his cheeks, and short, wavy, dark-blond hair. He had noticeably small ears but notably big hands. I like big hands. He evoked for me memories of the best of the corn-fed stock I grew to appreciate when I was going to college in Iowa.

How could this have happened? I am quite convinced that the dark masters of physical therapy, devising their sundry tortures in the shadowy depths of the hospital, would never knowingly send a therapist whom one might actually find pleasant—no doubt it would violate some law of reciprocal returns in physical therapy. Therefore I had to conclude that this masculine masterpiece was destined to work with some patient other than I, a patient who would find him suitably repulsive, difficult though that was to imagine. Alas—he looked to me like the perfect prescription for what ailed me: take two before bedtime and...maybe two more in the morning.

But maybe for all that he was a pill too large to swallow: once I had him in my nefarious clutches, just how much could I do with him? With one very gimpy leg I was hardly in a position to assume a position where any manner of athletic physical activity would be possible. Likewise, despite my most fervent desire, it was not going to be possible to fling my legs over his shoulders and enjoy with noisy and carefree abandon the tantalizing fruits of his loins. There would be no chance to discover in exactly how many ways this institution's ubiquitous latex gloves could be used to explore body cavities. Most unfortunately, it seemed likely that my abilities at that moment might extend only so far as a *Gedankenficken*— a "thought-fuck."

And then the morning formation was over, and the troops were dispersing to face their adversaries for the day. But wait! What was this? Contrary to all reasonable expectations and the wisdom of the Rolling Stones, sometimes you do get what you want. Incredibly, he, the cute one, the succulent vision, the stuff of wet dreams for weeks yet to come, was heading toward my room, determined and cheerful looking.

"Good morning, Mr. N. How are you and your leg doing this morning?" He pushed the door closed as he came through.

What a delight, I thought, *to dispense with all that "how are we" stuff so popular with so many of the health-care types.* It was almost startling, in fact, to be spoken to as though one had finally advanced into adulthood.

"Just fine, thank you. The pain is starting to recede, and I'm getting the earliest hint that some lateral motion in my leg is becoming possible again." He gave a good impression of actually listening.

"Excellent, excellent. My name is Marc..."

"Marc with a *c*?"

"Yes, with a *c*," he grinned, "and I'm your physical therapist for today. We won't be doing anything too awful, just trying to continue the good progress you've been making and getting some more mobility back into that leg."

His scrubs were a lovely teal-blue color that brought out his eyes. The V-neck in his scrubs also brought out his chest hair rather nicely. From the dense yet short and delicate hairs covering his arms, I thought I could reasonably extrapolate to a body-wide layer of fine, soft hair, something to brush gently with one's fingertips into pleasingly swirling patterns. Not to mention, of course, those large hands. I admit to a bit of difficulty paying attention to what Marc-with-a-*c* was saying, although it was great fun watching his lips move.

"Why don't we start by getting you into your chair?"

"Sounds like a plan to me."

The chair itself—a nondescript thing with arms and a cushion and a back that could recline—was the venue for most of my leg exercises. Getting into the chair was a significant enterprise that involved maneuvering me first into sitting at the edge of my bed, getting me into a standing position, moving my butt in the direction of the chair, and then lowering me into it. It wasn't a terribly graceful proposition.

We had gotten as far as my sitting at the edge of the bed. Marc paused and looked over the situation like he was having a brainstorm.

"We already know you can do the standing thing. How about today I lift you into your chair so you can save your energy for the exercises?"

It sounded good to me. I nodded hearty agreement.

"I'll lean over you and lock my arms under yours and around your back. Reach around my arms with your arms and hold on to my shoulders. I'll lift you up slowly and transfer you to the chair."

Again I nodded. This was a surprisingly intimate suggestion on his part in view of the fact the I was wearing only a pair of loose-fitting shorts. I easily overheated in hospital gowns and under warm blankets, but there's always one nurse with tightly pursed lips who finds it intolerably improper that one should be totally nude under one's own sheet, so I compromised with the shorts. Mind you, I found the intimacy of Marc's proposal a positive inducement. He leaned over me and I lifted my arms so he could encircle me with his arms. I felt his large hands clasp together behind my back and I tried not to moan aloud. His head next to mine, he spoke softly in my ear: "On three: one, two, three...."

He began to lift me up ever so gently. "Wait," I whispered back. I had a brainstorm of my own. He lowered me gently back, released his hold, and stood up.

"Was that causing pain?"

"No, that wasn't a problem at all. I was having trouble getting a good grip on your shoulders, that's all. I thought maybe if you took your top off...?"

Such audacity! Such presumption! Such impudence! Where did I ever find the reserve of nerve to ask this guileless young man to start disrobing right in front of me? I still can't believe that it came out of my mouth. What's more, I still can't believe that he did it.

Without demure he crossed his arms in front of his torso, grabbed the hem of his top, and lifted it up his body. I was enchanted as the tiny hairs on his abdomen brushed up and then lay back in place against his smooth skin. As he pulled, a delicious scent of lightly sunburned skin filled my nostrils. His rib cage expanded and lifted and then his small, dark-red nipples popped out from under the cloth. Fortunately his face was covered as the luxurious bushes under his armpits revealed themselves to my hungry gaze, otherwise I might have embarrassed him with the intensity of my interest.

He turned the thing right side out and laid it at the end of the bed. He didn't seem particularly bothered about being half naked with me. That I counted as a step forward.

We recommenced the transfer maneuver, skin to skin this time. Needless to say, my grip over his shoulders was firm and secure and my attention was undivided. As he lifted me up ever so gently, the flexing of his muscles tensed his pectorals, causing his nipples to perk up in the most inviting fashion, precariously close to my mouth. To avoid that oral temptation, I buried my face in his armpit and concentrated on breathing deeply and regularly. What a heavenly scent: agreeably acrid and musky, complex and masculine. I knew this scent from an early crush I had on one of those Iowa farm boys. It was an unexpected delight to enjoy it again.

I was in the chair and we were releasing our hold on each other, but not too quickly. I thought I detected—or imagined—a lingering tenderness, a slight desire on Marc's part to continue the physical contact. Surely a little imagination doesn't impede the physical therapy.

He leaned on the arms of the chair, his face close to mine. "I have one other patient to see this morning. Why don't you rest here for a while and I'll go see to her. That way, when I come back, I'll be all yours."

All mine sounded like a pretty good proposition. I nodded. Marc stood and tugged his top back on before he slipped out the door into the hallway. *Ah, well,* I thought, *one step forward, two steps backward.* Still, all mine. My eyes fell shut and I slept.

I evidently doze just long enough for Marc to finish with his other patient. Perhaps it's the sound of his softly closing the door to my room that wakes me. I watch through half-open

eyes as he moves quietly, first pulling off the top of his scrubs—
one step forward again!—then sitting on the floor in front of
me with his legs crossed. He lifts the foot of my gimpy leg
carefully into his lap. He holds it with the fingers of both his
big hands and massages around my toes.

"Mr. N., it's time for some leg exercises."

I open my eyes fully and nod.

"When I push and bend your foot toward you, use your
muscles to resist it."

We do twenty of those. I focus on his big, strong hands
while I flex my leg muscles.

"Good, good. Now the opposite: as I bend your foot toward
me, resist the motion."

Again with his big, strong hands! His fingers feel remarkably warm and comforting wrapped around my toes. How
unfortunate we only do twenty of those with each foot. I think
I could have done hundreds without getting tired or bored.

"Excellent. Next I'm going to lift your leg up a bit…."

I wince but for no good reason. His touch is sensitive and
nothing about it hurts.

"Now I'll support your lower leg and foot, and I'm going to
flex your thigh muscles by moving the foot first back toward
you, and then moving it forward toward me, just this slowly."

Toward me, toward Marc. Toward me, toward Marc. He
establishes a slow, steady rhythm that is almost hypnotic.
Toward me, toward Marc. My foot is right at the level of his
chest but I manage to avoid the strong temptation to tweak
his nipple with my big toe. Toward me, toward Marc, toward
me, toward Marc.

It feels good; can this be physical therapy? It is relaxing and
it loosens the thigh muscle in a good way. Here's the problem,

if it is a problem: the rhythmic motion is also sliding my shorts in syncopation up and down my other leg, arousing me very effectively, and my erection by this time is becoming rather insistent, not to mention quite evident visually. It's already peeking out a couple inches past the bottom of my shorts. Ah, well, Marc is a health professional, right? Seen it all before. Maybe he'll interpret it as positive body language.

Marc continues the rhythmic motion, nonplussed. "Personally, I always think that an erection is a good sign." (Toward me, toward Marc.) "It shows that the pain and discomfort are reducing enough"—toward me, toward Marc—"that you are coming back into contact with the rest of your body"—toward me, toward Marc—"and your feelings. Is this your first time since the surgery?"

"Yes it is. In fact, it's my first now in about three weeks."

"Excellent! In that case, we must celebrate!"

"Yes," I say, looking into his eyes, "we must definitely celebrate."

With no more warning than his smile, my big toe and its two nearest neighbors disappear into Marc's mouth. Oh, my beard! I have heard talk about this, but I am certain that I've never had my toes sucked before because I know I would have remembered. Who knew that one warm, wet, nubby tongue licking and caressing and probing between one's toes could feel so remarkably good? The tingling goes all the way up my leg, probably promoting more healing than all the leg exercises combined. Can one come through the toes? My passing thought is to hope that my ecstatic moans would be interpreted in the hallway as the wholly routine and nonsexual groans that usually accompany physical therapy. But I don't worry enough about it to stop.

The first-course shrimping cocktail ends all too soon, and I very narrowly avoid an orgasm from the appetizer! Marc continues to puff soft jets of breath over my still-wet toes, producing an indescribable cool-warm sensation. The effect is one of impish mischief.

"And now, Mr. N., what is your pleasure for the main course?"

"Alas, Marc, the condition of my leg precludes certain activities, but I don't think that need limit our fun. Sometimes it's best to return to basics and enjoy the simple pleasures, don't you think? I would very much like to suck you off, if you have no objection."

Marc voices none. He unfolds himself from sitting on the floor to standing and unties the knot in the cord around his waist. His scrub pants slip to the floor. He steps out of them and moves to the side of my chair. Vindication is mine when I see that, as I had hoped, his legs are indeed covered by the same dense, fine fur that adorns the rest of his body.

How fortunate for me that my chair puts my head precisely at the height of Marc's crotch. Somewhat too greedily, I run my hand firmly around his thigh, feeling the hair bristle beneath my fingers, feeling the shape of the muscle beneath Marc's smooth, malleable skin. I curve my hand around one cheek of his firm ass and pull his hips toward me.

At first I just bury my face in his crotch and breathe deeply of his clean, masculine scent. Yes, it is the same muskiness that I had become enamored of all those years ago. I drink it in. I extend my tongue and lick along the bottom of his balls, feeling their weight. In response, his still-soft dick twitches slightly against my cheek.

Pity all the poor people who are not cocksuckers—they

don't know what they're missing. The unique sensuality of a swollen dick slipping past one's lips, the head gliding over the roughness of one's tongue and just kissing the soft palate. The simple and satisfying oral gratification that so fires the imagination of Freudians. The unparalleled intimacy one feels at having another man's dick inside one's mouth.

I pull his dick into my mouth and hold it as it continues to swell, expanding and reaching for my throat. I swing my tongue back and forth against its underside in encouragement.

When his dick is fully hard, Marc slowly draws back, the shaft slipping out of my mouth just until the head reaches my lips, when he reverses and feeds himself slowly back into my mouth. I relax my jaw and keep my lips firmly around his dick, curling the tip of my tongue to tickle its head whenever it happens by.

With the same gentleness he showed with my leg, Marc thrusts his dick into my mouth with a slow, easygoing pace that is, once again, nearly hypnotic. I keep my hands on his thighs, fascinated by the alternating tensing then relaxing of the muscles as Marc fucks my face.

How long does this go on? Not long enough for me, given the incredible pleasure I am enjoying. But it is evidently just long enough for Marc. I feel his thigh muscles tensing more and his thrusts showing more suppressed urgency. Still greedy, I grab his ass and pull him hard against me so that his dick is buried deeply in my mouth. Marc locks his big hands around the back of my head and pulls it into his groin. My mouth is filled nearly to capacity, but I manage to tickle the underside of his dick with my tongue.

A small groan signals Marc's arrival and moments later I

am treated to spurt after spurt of his hot cum against the back of my throat. It's a remarkably satisfying sensation. There you go: yet another reason to be a cocksucker! I don't swallow, I just let his cum trickle down my throat.

All too soon, Marc's dick softens some and he pulls it from my mouth. However, he doesn't move very far, so I get to keep a close eye on it—and on his lovely balls as they slowly descend again—while Marc thoughtfully reaches down to stroke my achingly hard dick and relieve it of its burden. After this much stimulation, it takes but a few strokes before I shoot several loads up my belly, some reaching heights that I haven't known since adolescence.

We perform the necessary cleanup and Marc helps me back into bed, which now seems much more comfortable and restful than it had before. Thoughtfully, Marc does not pull his scrubs up again until we have finished all these chores so that I might retain the sweet image of his luscious body to help me sleep.

Before he leaves, Marc gives me a gentle kiss on the forehead and whispers, "Rest now and build up your strength, for tomorrow there will be more therapy and more healing."

I close my eyes and sleep.

DOWN THE BASEMENT

Ryan Field

One Halloween night during my senior year in college, I went to a costume party in a broken-down frat house, dressed as a character I'd been inventing for months—years, if you really want to get technical. I looked like any normal guy in college by then: short, sandy blond hair; blue eyes; white polo shirts and khaki slacks. Though I was only 5'6", there was nothing about me on the outside you would have considered peculiar. Most people would never have guessed that I was gay or that I had a secret passion for lipstick, earrings, and very high heels.

It's not that I didn't like being a man; I did and wouldn't have changed that for the world. But the thought of shaving my entire body to the point where every conceivable inch of skin was smooth and soft, and then putting on a tight corset, black stockings, and dangerous stilettos, gave me an erection that lasted for hours. Good sex for me was all about dressing up. All this was only fantasy, and though I'd once had the courage to buy a pair of cheap, size eleven, four-inch heels at Payless (buried at the bottom of my suitcase and only worn while I masturbated in private), I'd never actually had the guts to go out in public dressed as a slutty woman.

Not until the night of the costume party, anyway. I wasn't cruising for guys, either; I just wanted to dress up and feel sexy for once. I'd spent months ordering the most precise items on the Internet, things I knew would make me appear and feel really hot. The general costume consisted of a black, beaded evening bag; a short black taffeta skirt; a skintight, black lace corset trimmed in silver; a black mask that covered half my face; and six-inch black stilettos. But it was the small details that really made the costume work: rhinestone earrings, necklace and bracelet; long, red fake fingernails; full makeup; and a pair of vinyl boobs, with big nipples, that felt real when you squeezed them. I'd signed up at a tanning salon a month before the party so my legs would be smooth and brown...no need for stockings. And, best of all, a long blonde wig with a snug fit so I could toss my head around without worrying about losing it.

Actually, my only real worry was holding my eight-inch penis down all night. I found a strong black thong-sock (no string, so my ass would be bare) with a heavy waistband to keep things concealed. I knew if I got really hard I could point my dick toward my stomach and the waistband would hold it down. Though I made a few mistakes (didn't need eye makeup with a mask...when the wig was on my head I realized all I needed was a little red lip gloss to pass), my first time going out in public I looked quite professional. And it was *supposed* to be outrageous; this was a costume party, after all.

The high heels made me feel sexual and powerful, and as I strutted across campus to the frat house party a couple of guys turned to stare at my bare legs. They weren't the best-looking boys on campus, but they were real men—they were pussy hounds and they liked the way I looked. I concentrated very carefully on my movements so that I wouldn't appear masculine. I didn't want to come off as quasi feminine, either, so I simply restricted each movement to avoid anything awkward or too calculated. Then I smiled and said, "Hey, guys." The tall dude, a horny African American, said, "Yeah, sweet baby, where you been all my life?"

I told him, "Going to meet my boyfriend, sweetie." He laughed, and while I continued to walk away, I heard him tell his friend, "I'd like to get me a piece of that sugar, man. I know how to make her happy." If I'd had any doubts about being able to pass as a woman, those two boys proved I could do it as long as I was careful.

The costume was a huge hit, and no one recognized me or even considered I might not be a woman. No one from my usual crowd was there, anyway; I was an English major, and these people were all jocks and cheerleaders. I was glad I'd worn the sock underwear; my dick was semierect the entire time, especially when I realized that young guys were staring at my legs. But the goal was to have fun passing as a woman for the first time, nothing more. And if for some reason I was recognized by anyone, I knew I could camp it up as a man in drag, just wearing an outrageous Halloween costume for fun.

Some of the other costumes were good, too: a kinky witch

(I think she was a real woman) with big boobs in black leather and lace, a scarecrow who was actually smoking from the shoulders, one really swishy gay guy dressed as Baby Jane Hudson, and a guy with a realistic Richard Nixon mask are a few that still come to mind. But others weren't all that creative, like the guys with deep voices who didn't bother to come up with a real costume and just wore their football uniforms with black masks.

It turned out to be one of those parties where you don't really have to know anyone very well to have a good time, and because it was a costume party people seemed more animated behind their masks. I laughed and joked with Baby Jane Hudson, while Richard Nixon kept bringing me strong drinks and trying to put his hand up my little black skirt. At one point, with the palm of his hand pressed against my ass, he leaned over and whispered, "My car is parked outside."

And I replied, "Sorry, stud, I have a boyfriend." He was cool about it and didn't persist. I would have loved to at least given him a blow job, only I was terrified he'd find out who I really was and kick my ass.

We all partied hard, mixing beer and whatever else there was, all night long. Sometime around two in the morning, one of the drunken football players reached behind me while I was leaning against a wide oak staircase and placed the palm of his large hand up my skirt, resting it on my bare ass. His pale blue eyes were eager; one eyebrow rose for the conquest. He squeezed my asscheeks and said, "Those fucking high heels are really hot." He was about 6'4", and towered over me in spite of the stilettos; his words were slurred and his breath heavy and stale from beer when he asked, "Why aren't you wearing any underwear?"

"So you can put your hand up my dress, sweetie, and feel my ass." I couldn't believe my own words, but there, I'd said it.

He then asked if I wanted to go down to the basement recreation room, to smoke a joint with three of his football buddies. I agreed, and he nodded to his buddies who must have been waiting for a signal. He led me downstairs with his large hand pressed against the small of my back as though I belonged to him.

The basement was dark, with just two dim lightbulbs with pull strings, and I had to navigate with care because of the high heels. A dusty old braided rug had been placed in the center of the concrete floor; my heels sank into the grooves. A large sectional sofa with worn navy fabric and a square, dark pine coffee table with heavy, turned legs rested upon the stained rug. The football player told me, "Have a seat, baby," while he pulled a small bag from beneath a sofa cushion and proceeded to roll a joint on the table. I put the black evening bag on the table, sat in the middle of the sofa, and crossed my legs like a lady. A moment later, I heard the sound of heavy footsteps clomping down the stairs—his three football buddies, I assumed. Though I had to clench my fists to keep them from shaking, the thought of three strong football players with big floppy dicks who were all hot for me caused my ass to literally twitch.

They were so drunk they couldn't stand straight. They were joking and laughing and shoving each other around playfully, saying things in deep voices like, "Get the fuck out of here, dude," and, "Fuck, yeah, man, you pussy." Bad little locker room boys with too much testosterone, having too much fun at a party in front of a slutty young girl who was showing too much leg that night. One still held a bottle of vodka in his right hand. I knew none of them would ask me to the senior prom, but I also knew they wanted to get into my pants in the worst way. Though I'd been drinking, I was far from drunk and calculated my every move very carefully. I knew if they found me out they'd beat me to a pulp, and by then it was too late to leave gracefully.

"C'mon over here and sit on my lap, so I can take off that mask," said the football player who'd brought me down to the basement. He'd removed his mask by then and was smoking the joint, about to pass it to one of his buddies.

Two of them sat down on my right, the third on my left. They were quiet by then, but their eyes were eager and their expressions blank, not sure who would make the first move. None were wearing masks; they'd probably lost them upstairs somewhere.

I smiled. "I want to smoke first." I leaned over, pressed my palm on the upper thigh of the guy next to me, while he held the joint and I took a long drag. I knew if we all got stoned, and they got so wasted they didn't know what day of the week it was, I wouldn't have to worry about being discovered.

The one who wanted me on his lap, the leader of the pack, stood and walked over to a bookcase with a large television and one of those small Bose radios. He turned on the radio and turned up the volume, and Mary K. Blige began to sing. "Let's dance," he said, grabbing my hand and pulling me off the sofa.

The other three, still passing the joint around, howled, "Go man, yeah, look at her move."

I fell into his strapping body and placed my arms around his wide shoulders. He pulled me closer, and then put his rough hands under my dress and lifted it all the way up to my waist so the other guys could see him petting my bare ass. We began to dance very slowly; I arched my back and invited him to play with my asscheeks while I rubbed the back of his thick neck. His breath smelled like pot and beer; I slowly licked the stubble below his ear, and he moaned. One of the guys on the sofa, a tall, lanky dude with huge hands, stood and staggered up behind me. He put his hands around my waist, shoved his crotch against my ass and began to slowly hump, his erection banging against my crack. I reached down with my right hand and began to massage the one in front; his erection was so hard and thick I felt it pulse through the fabric of his football pants. He leaned forward and stuck his tongue in my mouth while the one behind me reached down and began to gently squeeze my ass.

I knew I had to change course; his next drunken move would be to reach between my legs for a pussy that wasn't there. So I untangled myself from the sandwich and said, "Okay, boys, everyone on the sofa."

They were eager to please; the joint was finished, and they were all too wasted to remember anything by that point. The leader, who'd brought me down there in the first place, sat off to the side at the edge of the sofa and watched; the other three sat next to each other. I slowly went down on my knees and began to unlace the football pants of the one who had been behind me dancing. I pulled his pants down to his knees; a nine-inch erection popped out because he wasn't wearing underwear. I removed his shoes and pulled his pants off altogether. While he moaned, and the others grabbed their crotches, I ran my long red fingernails up his dark hairy legs, took hold of the erection and began to slurp and suck as though I hadn't been fed dick in years. He tasted salty and smelled like vinegar and cheese because his balls had been sweating during the party. With my dark-red lips wrapped around the head, I began to jerk the shaft with my right hand. He blew a load into my mouth within minutes, and I gulped the whole thing and sucked out the last drops so there wouldn't be any mess.

I wasted no time in repeating the same act with the guy sitting next to him, which took even less time (horny, drunk boys get off fast, I learned). But when I reached the third, who had already pulled his dick out for me, the leader at the edge of the sofa leaned over and whispered, "I want to fuck you, baby."

My eyes bugged as though I'd been caught with my hand in the cookie jar, and he seemed to sense the fear.

"Don't worry," he whispered, "I know you're not a girl. I knew it when I asked you to come down the basement. I just wanna fuck you, please."

"But what about him?" Though the first two were already snoring, the third guy with heavy, glazed eyes waited for his blow job, too. His dick stood out from the opening of the football pants, and he was jerking off. He was slightly over-weight (the linebacker type) but had really sexy, sloppy bull-sized balls I couldn't wait to lick.

"Just get up, lean over the arm of the sofa, and spread your legs," he said. "You can suck him off while I bang you. I know you want it."

We both stood, while the last guy watched as though he couldn't predict what would happen next, and I leaned over the arm of the sofa and wrapped my red lips around the head of his cock. He didn't care what happened after that; he only wanted to get sucked off so he could go to sleep, too. His dick was curved and long—not as thick as the first guy and not as sweet as the second, but I couldn't help liking the way it hit the back of my throat when I sucked all the way down to his sour ball sac. It occurred to me that I was even more turned on now that the leader knew I was really a guy.

While I sucked the third guy off, the leader pulled his fat cock out, lifted my black taffeta skirt up to my waist, and spread my asscheeks. He blew a huge wad of spit; it hit my hole and he pressed the head of his dick against it. He rolled the head around for a moment to lube me and then slowly inserted the tip. I arched my back and spread my legs; he grabbed my knees and lifted them with both hands so that he could pound away. With my legs bent at the knees and high heels in the air, he fucked me like a machine, and I moaned and continued to suck off the football player on the sofa. The harder the one behind me hammered, the harder I sucked the cock in my mouth.

Again, it didn't take long for either of them to reach climax. But something happened to me, too, that I hadn't expected. The one behind me began to hit a sensitive spot, and my orgasm began to rise. And as the guy on the sofa grabbed the back of my blonde wig to let me know he was coming, the one behind me blew his load up my hole, and I shot my load into the black thong. While I slurped up and swallowed the last drops from guy number three, and the leader was still depositing his last drops of seed up my ass, I marveled at how I'd had an orgasm without touching myself. He remained inside for a few moments while I gently licked the third guy's sloppy ball sac.

Then he pulled out fast, helped me to my feet, and offered another drink. The others were passed out; the minute I started to lick and suck the third guy's balls, he too had begun to snore.

"Why not," I said, taking a couple of long swigs from the bottle of vodka. He put his arm around my waist and pulled me to his chest, drops of him now trickling down my bare legs...as the room began to spin.

"You certainly do deserve it," said the leader. "You worked hard tonight."

I smiled, but nearly lost my balance; the last drink of vodka had now put me over the edge, too. "You were wonderful. You made me come without touching my dick." I reached down and cupped his dick and balls in my hand.

"You have a great hole, baby," he said

I passed out right after that and don't remember anything until I woke up about three hours later, facedown across two snoring football players who wore nothing but jockstraps; one great athletic hand was resting on the middle of my ass...my face pressed to the crook of a hairy ball sac. Though I did take a couple of quick sniffs, and the tip of my tongue couldn't help licking the guy's tangy sac for a few minutes, I suddenly became terrified they would wake up and beat the shit out of me. I slowly rose, while the guys continued to snore, and searched for my black beaded bag. The basement was dark; I couldn't find it anywhere.

A deep football player voice said, "Looking for this?" His eyes were heavy as he waved my bag in the air.

"Ah, yes," I said, still trying to remember everything that had happened that night.

He handed me the bag. "No kiss good-bye?"

I looked at him and smirked. I'd just remembered he was the kinky boy who knew I wasn't a woman. "Why didn't you beat the shit out of me last night?"

"They really thought you were a girl, and I'm into it—chicks with dicks," he said, trying hard to speak clearly. "Last night was really hot, man...maybe we could hook up again sometime, just you and me."

I reached into my bag, pulled out a card with my email address, and handed it to him. "But the ball is in your court, buddy," I said. "This could be a once-in-a-lifetime thing for me. I don't usually do this, and I'm not sure I ever will again. Just wanted to have a little fun on Halloween."

He smiled, and then put his hand up my dress. "I'll get in touch. This can be our little secret. But next time I want to see you in red high heels with a red garter belt."

I leaned forward and kissed him good-bye. He put his hand up my dress one more time, and then I quietly left while the other football players were still sleeping.

A ROOFER'S WORK

Shane Allison

When wet chunks of sheet rock fell from the
ceiling of our Pepto-pink bedroom, Rashaan
was pissed, and vowed it was the final straw.
We were fed up with putting buckets and pans
under cracks in the ceiling where brown rainwater seeped in through worn shingles and
plywood, soaking the carpet, giving the entire
house a rank mildew smell, an aura of dank-
ness. Because of all the work that needed to
be done, our relationship was strained. It was
going to cost us thousands in repairs, plus
remodeling the kitchen and overhauling the
old toilets. You can't live in Hurricane Country
with a bad roof. Florida had four last year,
back to back.

Rashaan used to greet me with a blow job
every morning; now he's out the door before I

am. Our sex life is soggier than the house. I give myself hand
jobs between cloaking the holes with black sheets of plastic
and duct-taping leaks.

I finally convinced Rashaan that Sammie, our neighbor, an
all-around Mr. Fix-it, could come over and repair the roof.
Rashaan had been adamantly opposed, saying, "'On' want
these nosy black folks knowin' our business."

I've known these so-called nosy black folks all my life. Mr.
Freddy used to take me to school if I missed the bus. I used
to buy grape frozen cups from Mrs. Emma up the road for
ten cents. I played basketball with Lynwood before he started
boozin'.

Sammie does everything from cutting down rotted tree limbs
to overhauling car engines. He used to work with my daddy
doing odd jobs for old ladies. He has a sanctified wife and two
kids, a son in grade school and a daughter at Rickards High.

I should have hired someone who didn't live in such close
proximity, someone who didn't know us, after all. But how
was I supposed to know Sammie and me would end up messing
around? I'm no psychic, and I sure as shit don't have a crystal
ball in my pocket.

The morning Sammie arrived, he startled me out of a dream,
which I didn't mind so much considering most of them are
bizarre. It was around nine-ish, way too early for someone
who had worked two shifts at CVS the night before. I squinted
at the beams of light that poured through the verticals of the
den's windows.

"Somebody's at th' door, 'Shaan."

I looked around with crusts of sleep in my eyes. The only
sign of Rashaan was a wet towel from his morning shower
and a cold, half-empty cup of black coffee sitting on the table,

with no sign of a coaster beneath it. I stumbled into the living room.

"Ow. Fuck!" I yelled. I'd stubbed my big toe against the metal leg of the coffee table. It throbbed as I limped to the door. The cold linoleum in the built-in porch was freezing beneath my feet. I sported a hard-on 'cause I hadn't taken my morning piss. It was a bitch to keep restrained in my boxers. I usually don't wear them 'cause they ride up in the crack of my ass and don't provide any support for my package, unlike the snug of undies.

I opened the door and squinted again at the cruel light. With my blurred vision, I could barely make out that it was Sammie on my doorstep, dressed in a T-shirt with cutoff Dickies. The white van with SOUTHERN FIXIN'S painted on the side in a large, blue, fancy font, was a clue. Sammie is the hottest hunk in Woodville, nothing like the tobacco-spitting, dick-grabbing Confederate rednecks and store corner drunkards who populate the place.

"Wa'sup," he said in his Southern-fried baritone. "Charlynn gave me ya message 'bout th' roof leakin'."

"Yeah, th' shingles in th' garage." I stumble-stepped over a row of boxwoods and hoisted up the garage door—something else we have on our "Fix This" list. The shingles were stacked between the lawnmower and the Weedwhacker, both of which Rashaan and I rarely used.

Sammie bent to retrieve the first stack of shingles, giving me a swell view of his ass. I knew they weighed a ton. I used to help Daddy unload them off his truck.

"Ya need some help?" I asked.

"Naw, I got it." Last thing I wanted to do was help him haul those damn things up a twelve-foot ladder. I was fine gawking at his ass, the glistening Dutch-chocolate muscles of his arms. Droplets of dry tar tarnished his boots. I don't think I'd ever seen him clothed from the waist up before. He was usually shirtless, cut and sweaty, either mowing his yard or tinkering around under the hood of someone's candy-painted Cadillac. Sammie would come up for air caked in motor oil, looking like something out of a Herb Ritts photo.

It never occurred to me that he was into guys. I mean, here was a dude who lifted weights and held pit bull fights.

I left him at his job to go drain my dick before I had to perform my version of the pee-pee dance. On my way to the john, I spotted a note on the coffee table where I'd stubbed my toe, written on pink paper: *Gone to grocery store, be back in an hour, love, Rashaan.*

As I milked my dick, the doorbell rang again.

"Fuck, what is it now?" I muttered. I tried to speed things up, but you can't rush a pee. "U'm comin'," I yelled. I tapped the last droplets from my dick and pushed it back into the plaid slit. I missed Rashaan's blow jobs at the crack of dawn.

"Hey, sorry t' botha ya, but can I trouble ya fuh a glass of wata?"

"Oh, my bad, man. Come on in. I should've asked if ya wanted some t' drink."

The door was rotting off the hinges due to rainwater and termites. Sammie stepped in and wiped his feet on the flower welcome mat. He already reeked like a brute.

"I don't think I've been here since ya mama an' daddy died," he said.

"Sorry 'bout th' mess," I said. Rashaan had left the air conditioner on through the night, so at least the house was cool. Sammie trekked behind me, through the den, to the kitchen.

He pulled a chair from the table and took a seat.

"I got beer, wata, juice, an' ice tea."

"Tea is good."

I pushed past the bottles of Corona, Orange Ocean fruit punch, and expired low-fat chocolate milk, slid the pitcher of sweet tea out of the fridge, and set it on the counter. I opened the cabinet, reaching past sandwich plates, cereal bowls, and pie saucers, and grabbed the tallest glass I could find.

"Ya want ice?" I asked.

"Yeah, that's fine. I like t' suck on th' cubes."

My dick rose to his words. I prayed it wouldn't show itself. I poured until I filled the glass to its rim with tea.

"Gettin' hot out there?" I asked, dropping in ice cubes.

"Damn hot. Not hot. Damn hot." He laughed.

"'On' know how ya do dat kinda work every day."

"There's good money in roofin'," he said, after a gulp of tea. I grabbed the last Sunny D for myself from behind leftover pepperoni pizza.

"Yoon get scared up there on them roofs?"

"U'm use to it," he said, looking at me. I looked back, before my gaze dropped to his bulge. My own dick swelled. I've always wondered about Sammie's size. Growing up, I use to fantasize about having sex with him, that country dick up my ass.

Good thing I was sitting down. I didn't want Sammie to know that he was responsible for my sudden hard-on. Sweat trickled down his goose-bumped neck as he drank the tea, cubes kissing his lips. My erection could have been avoided if Rashaan had blown me instead of running off to buy TV dinners, his favorite food, even though I warn him that if he gets fat I'll leave his ass.

Sammie drank the rest of the tea and set the glass on the table.

"Can I use ya bathroom?" he asked as he rubbed his hands along his thighs, drying off condensation.

"Lemme show ya where it's at."

He followed me through the living room and the den. I could feel his eyes on my ass.

"It's right through dat door."

"'Preciate it." Sammie patted me on the back, but a love tap on the butt would've been better.

Rashaan was always saying he'd be gone for an hour, but it was always more like two or three—or all day. As I watched cardinals fluttering around the yard through the den window, I listened to Sammie's piss splash. The door was slightly ajar. Sammie was silhouetted against the white shower curtain, with pastel butterfly prints Rashaan had picked out at Bed Bath & Beyond. His dick was cloaked by an uncut sheath that glistened with sweat beneath the bathroom light.

The last uncut dick I'd sucked was attached to Kevin, a substitute teacher who left the worst taste in my mouth. After him, I swore never again, no more uncut skin.

Sammie flushed the toilet then came out fastening his shorts. I asked him how often he worked out, hoping he hadn't noticed my Peeping Tom-foolery.

"'Bout six times a week. Why?"

I told him I wished I had a body like his. He stood towering, over me like a Southern Hercules. Sammie asked if I had any weights.

"Th' only thing I have is an exercise bike I bought from th' flea market. I wanna build up muscle mass," I told him.

"Then ya need t' getcha some weights."

I asked if I could feel his muscles.

"Go 'head." His biceps were as hard as sledges. One was branded with a Greek symbol from some kind of fraternity.

"Where you went t' school?" I asked, as I squeezed his guns.

Sammie told me that he was a graphic arts major at Howard University.

"So what happened?"

"I had t' quit, 'cause I couldn't afford th' tuition, so I came back t' Tallahassee an' got a job movin' furniture t' save some money fuh school, but it ain' pay nothin'. Lynwood hooked me up wit dis roofin' job. They pay thirty dollars an hour."

"How long ya been workin' there?" I asked

"Fo' years."

Dirty thoughts of his dick were dancing in my head. Leaky roofs, shingles, and even Rashaan were the last things I was thinking about. He tugged at his package. "Well, lemme get back t' work."

"Lemme know if ya need anything."

As I cleaned the kitchen, scrubbing burnt skin from last night's baked chicken off the roasting pan, I could hear Sammie. His goose steps on the roof were thunderous—an unearthly invasion. Bored by the kitchen cleaning, I went out to see if he needed anything. It was almost noon and hot as hell. I walked to the side of the house where the ladder stood.

"How's it goin' up there?" I hollered. No answer.

I figured he couldn't hear me with all the hammering. I decided to climb to the roof, even though I was hardly dressed for clambering up ladders. I was halfway up when it started to slide along the edge of the roof.

"Sammie!" I yelled. The sun burned my eyes. His body blocked it.

"Wha'choo doin'?" he laughed.

"Man, help me up. This thing's 'bout t' fall."

"Gimme ya han'," Sammie said.

The ladder kept giving as I reached up for him.

"U'ma fall." I told him.

"You ain' go'n fall. Jus' reach up," he said. I was scared to let go.

"C'mon, I gotcha." I finally entrusted myself to him.

"Pull me up," I begged. Sammy grabbed my arms and hauled me over the brink of the roof. I clutched him as I made my way to safety. Just in time, too. The ladder crashed to the driveway below. I was scared shitless, life flashing, kissing my ass good-bye, and all that.

"You all right?" Sammie asked.

Hell no ain' all right, I thought. "Yeah, I jus' need t' catch my breath," I said. "You ain' hear me callin' you?"

"Uh-uh, no."

We looked to the ground at the fallen ladder.

"How we go'n get down?" I asked.

"I'll jus' push ya off th' roof t' get th' ladda," he joked.

"An' yo' ass'll be goin' down wit me." I laughed.

"Since ya up here, ya might as well gimme a han'."

I wasn't much for that kind of work. As a teen, I spent summers helping Daddy build utility buildings. Hauling lumber and catching splinters in my hands wasn't my idea of a summer vacation.

"Grab some of dis felt paper." I held the roll of black covering while he pulled a tongue of the tough stuff across the roof. My shirt was already drenched. Sweat trickled down the ditch of my ass. My glasses slid off my face, I pushed them back to the bridge of my nose, they slid down again.

"Grab that hammer right there and some of them nails, and nail yo' en' down fuh me," said Sammie.

"Where th' nails at?" I asked.

"Them right dere."

I took a nail and held it to one corner of the black paper, steadied it, drew back my hammer, and…"Ow, fuck!" I hollered as I smashed my finger. I swear all of Woodville must have heard me. My bruised toe twitched in sympathy.

"You all right?"

As I attempted to suck the pain away, blood started to pool under the bed of my fingernail.

"Lemme see."

"Fuck, it hurt," I said.

Sammie took my hand into his.

"Ya go'n haff t' get dat blood drained from unda dere," he said.

"Uh-uh, that shit go'n hurt."

"It ain't go'n hurt. I think I hava safety pin in my toolbox."

I suckled my finger to cool the pain.

"Don't be sucha baby, man." I looked away squeamishly just as he was about to press the needle end of the pin under my nail bed.

It hurt like hell as he made the prick.

"Ya done yet?" I asked, not quite whimpering.

"Yeah, le' me ge'choo some t' wrap it in." My finger felt like the devil's asshole. Sammie wrapped my wound in a ripped piece of drop cloth. "Jus' make sure ya let all th' blood drain out."

This is why we always call somebody to do the handy work, 'cause between me and Rashaan, neither one of us knows a band saw from a chainsaw. But I wasn't about to let a damn hammer get the best of me.

"Wha'choo doin?"

"What it look like?" I was starting to swing the hammer again.

"Here, lemme show ya," he said, taking the hammer. He squatted down next to me, leaning in close. Our skin kissed. Droplets of sweat plummeted from his brow.

"Hol' it like this at th' en' of th' handle keepin' all th' weight on th' steel en'. Tap th' nail t' get it started an'..." Sammie tapped in the nail with one stroke. The grease from his hair cooked in the July heat.

"Want me t' start anotha one fuh ya?"

"I thank I got it." He watched me nonetheless, standing over me, shirtless, glazed with sweat. I wanted to lick the tips of his steel toe kickers, kiss the boot strings, run my tongue up his steel calves and sturdy thighs, past his dick and up the ridge of his abs, onto his thick pecs. Instead, I hammered, and after I'd proven that I had the hang of things, he attended to his own work. Sammie's tool belt hung low, tugging down his cutoffs so a sliver of ass crack was exposed. My dick fattened to every dirty thought that formed while every other muscle in me ached. Here I was talking about Rashaan, and I needed to lay off the cookies and chips my damn self.

"How ya doin' down here?" Sammie asked.

"You tell me." He studied my work.

"Pretty good," he said. Sammie helped me to nail the rest of the felt paper and start the shingles. As we worked, he asked, "Where Rashaan at?"

"He went to th' store t' get some groceries. He been gone since dis mornin'."

"You ain' haff t' work t'day?" Sammie asked.

"U'm off till Thursday. U'm tryin' t' use up all my sick leave."

"Hey, if I ask ya some, ya promise not t' get mad?"

"Wa'sup?"

"Who play th' man an' who play th' woman?" asked Sammie.

"Who play th' man?" I laughed.

"Wi'choo an' Rashaan."

If I had a dime for every time somebody asked me that, I'd be featured on "MTV Cribs."

"Who ya think?" I grinned.

"'On' know. I guess you be on th' bottom," he said.

"Why ya say dat?"

"'Cause you mo' feminine an' Rashaan act mo' like...th' nigga."

"We 'on' do nonna dat role playin' shit. Sometimes I get fucked, sometimes he do."

"Dat's wa'sup," Sammie said.

We went back to our work laying shingles, nailing down roofing paper.

"Do it hurt?" Sammie asked.

"What hurt?"

"Gettin' fucked."

He was getting personal, but I was never one to skate around hot sex talk.

"In th' beginnin', yeah. Ya jus' gotta relax. After a few times, it jus' slips in." When he asked about my dick size, he proved that he had brass balls, but so did I.

"How big are you?"

"Probably 'bout seven inches," said Sammie, after a pause. "I ain' measured since high school." We had half the roof covered. "Le's take a break. I gotta pee."

He walked to the brink of the roof. Sammie slid his tool belt around his waist. "Dat tea runnin' clean through me," he said. I studied his stream of gold plummeting off the house my parents had left me.

"Ya better go'n head an' go, 'cause I wanna get most of th' shingles down befo' th' day ova wit."

"U'm scareda heights," I told him.

"I hear dat lie," he laughed. "C'mon, don't be a pussy." I took my place next to him. I forked it out of my plaid slit, and our pee rained from the roof. We looked to the trees, squirrels scurrying along the trunks of great oaks. I peeked at his stuff peripherally. He was modest about his size. Sammie moved in closer. His boots touched my flip-flops, our arms kissed again. It shocked me when he reached over to grab my dick.

"Uh-uh, for boyfriends only," I teased. We shook the remaining drops from our slits.

"What about all dem guys dat be in an' outta here?"

"Wha'choo go'n do, tell Rashaan?"

"I see how ya be lookin' at me when ya drive by."

"Don't nobody be lookin' a'choo," I laughed.

"Watchin' me work out."

It was true. I would practically slow to a crawl just to get a look at his fine ass. I mean shit, just because I'm with somebody, don't mean I can't look.

"But it's all good. Ain' got no problem wi'chall watchin'."

"Ya'll?" I said.

"I catch Rashaan starin' sometimes."

I wasn't surprised. He's always had a wandering eye.

"U'm done up here. I wanna get down," I told him.

"You ain' go'n help me wit th' rest of th' shingles?"

"U'm payin' you t' do all dis rememba? Plus u'm tied an' I wanna put somethin' on my finga."

"Did I make ya uncomfortable askin' ya dat about Rashaan?"

"It ain't dat. I's jus' hot up here."

Sammie went for my dick again.

"Stop playin'," I laughed, shielding my privates. I stank and was sweaty, and all I wanted to do was take a bath.

"I saw ya watchin' me in th' bathroom."

My heart fluttered with embarrassment.

"I tol' joo it's cool," he said. Sammie ran his fingers along the impression of his dick, back in his cutoffs.

"I wanna get down," I said.

"If ya' suck my dick I'll get us from up here."

"You shittin' me, right?"

"Ya'll can suck a mean dick."

That sounded like he had dipped his toes in these waters before.

"I don't want Rashaan t' catch us," I said.

"You said he go'n be gone fuh hours." Sammie pulled his shirt up, exposing his torso. My dick was hard and hot.

"Somebody might see us up here," I said.

"Nothin' but th' birds."

I let my dick pop from the slit of my loose boxers. Sammie studied my excitement. He fished his out and roped his fingers around its girth.

"U'ma push ya off dis shit myself if yo'on get me down," I said, playing hard to get. Sammie sat against the piping that led down to the wood stove in the house. The summer was cooking us. Sweat rolled into the crease of my mouth. Sammie pulled at his dick. There was a fine brunet bush at the base. Musky. Just as I was about to go for his dick, Sammie stopped me. "Get in between my legs." He flung off his filthy tee and took down his Dickies, leaving nothing but those tar-spotted boots. I worshipped and licked them.

"Look up at me," he said. Sammie smelled dirty, tasted salty. He started to pivot.

"Breathe through your nose." Sammie pushed me down on it. The aggressive type. I gagged. My body wanted to purge this roofer's dick from my mouth.

"Use ya hand," he demanded. I pushed down and pulled up on his sheath.

"Dis how Charlynn do it?" I asked.

"She 'on' suck. Talkin' 'bout i's a sin. Now that she sancti-fied, she 'on' wanna fuck."

I wasn't surprised. She didn't look like the dick-sucking type.

"Lick my balls." I lapped at scrotum skin but Sammie objected when I tried to work a finger up his ass.

"'On' get down like dat." Typical. He was a nice guy, but he was one of these breeders who thinks if he doesn't take it up the ass or throw his lips to a dick, he's not a punk. I worked at his cock and balls, hoping to keep his mind off my wandering finger. Sammie protested again. "I tol' joo 'on' get fucked. U'ma real man."

"I'll put it in jus' a lil' bit." I lubed my finger with spit and went for him a third, charmed time. I started slow. Sweat blurred and burned. He didn't object this time. I studied his face as I went in steady, deep. He wasn't as tight as I thought, which made me wonder if he really was a stranger to getting nailed. Sammie worked his dick as I finger-fucked him. I hoped that Rashaan was taking his time at the grocery store pondering fresh vegetables versus frozen.

"Stop," said Sammie. "Ain' ready t' come yet. My turn."

I told him that I had some rubbers in the house.

"I'll pull out befo' I come," he said.

"'On' know," I objected.

"Ain' got no diseases or nothin'," Sammie said. "Get on ya back. I wanna look a'choo." He hooked fingers in my boxers, tugging them down from my ass. He pulled me to him with strong, scarred hands. He spat into his right one and then slathered it on his dick. He pried me wide, ass already wet with the heat of the day.

I thought I was ready for anything till he shoved it in. It hurt. He was bigger than what I was used to. He was heavy and filthy on top of me, thrusting his love up my butt under a sky of cotton candy clouds, a butterscotch sun. Sammie was a beast as he took me.

"Yeah, Charley!" he yelled. I figured this was his nickname for Charlynn. I swiped at my eyes to keep the sweat out. Sammie was giving Rashaan a run for his money. I was getting close as I worked my dick. Sammie's thrusts began to slow.

"U'mma come!"

I felt him pull out. His dick sputtered semen across my belly. He reached under and finished me off until I came on myself. Sammie's fingers were stained with my stuff. The two of us sprawled, spent. We made ourselves decent, pushing arms back into filthy T-shirts, legs into shorts and boxers; he adjusted his tool belt, I tucked away my tool.

"How we go'n get down?" I asked.

"I'll jump fuh it."

"An' you go'n break ya neck," I said.

Sammie leaped, landing in a pile of leaves below. He leaned the ladder against the house for my rescue.

"Hol' it while I climb down."

I felt for each rung with my feet.

"You got it?"

"Jus' come on off th' ladda," Sammie said.

I was relieved when both feet hit solid ground. "I'll live," I laughed.

"Of course you will...I'll jus' leave my tools an' stuff up dere fuh tomorrow," said Sammie.

"How long iz it go'n take ya t' fix?" I asked.

"No reason why I shouldn't be done by Sunday. Ya wanna help me out again tomorrow?"

"Rashaan'll be at work, so I should be able t' give ya a han'."

Rashaan was barreling around the corner as Sammie backed out.

"Hey, baby," he said, pulling bags of groceries out of the trunk after Sammie cleared the driveway and he drove in.

"Wha' joo get?" I asked, taking the groceries out of his arms.

HEATED

Vincent Diamond

When the station siren blared, I was right in the middle of adding the five-pound can of tomatoes to the chili; a tricky maneuver, trying not to splash too much. The new cooktop gleamed and we were all trying—not very successfully—to keep it in good shape. It had taken years for the county to spring for a new one.

As the siren faded away, I tabbed the cooktop to OFF and ran down to my gear. Eight guys jumping onto two engines make for a lot of noise so I barely heard the address as Jesse and I clambered into my Lieutenant's truck. It was dark already, seven o'clock on a December night in Florida. Cool and clear and dry. Prime fire weather.

Jesse tapped his cell phone, paging through the county appraiser's website. "Let's see, Pine

Tree Lane? Oh, here we go. Hidden Pines Equestrian Center. Two mobile homes on the property, a concrete block storage unit and a barn." His thumbs tapped the little keyboard. We teased Jesse about his gadget jones but there were times it came in handy. "Last tax roll says eighteen stalls."

Which could mean eighteen—or more—panicked horses. And their owners.

Fuck.

Four minutes later, we could see the smoke. Two minutes after that, we pulled onto the gravel road that led to the horse farm and saw the flames. Low-hanging branches scraped the top of the truck but even over that noise, we heard the horses.

Screaming.

Shadowed figures ran through the darkness, some four-legged, some two-legged. The engine in front of us braked hard when a horse ran in front of it, maybe not fast enough; there was a thump but that could have been a tire on a tree branch. We couldn't tell if it glanced off the horse or not.

Once we parked, we all had a job to do, getting the hoses out, hooking up the water, scoping out the power lines, skimming the fire retardant, double-checking one another's gear. We don't do much yelling; it's not like on TV with a bunch of screaming and hollering. We talk when we have to but once our respirators are on, it's hard to understand someone, especially over the roar of a big fire.

The barn was laid out in a *T*. The stalls at the top of the *T* were already empty, their doors swinging open. But it was the hallway toward the back that had all the action: people yelling, horses whinnying and screaming, and fire eating up the back end of the barn like a kid chomping on cotton candy.

There were five civvies on-site when we got there. All of them scrambled around, leading horses, waving their arms, covering the horses' eyes, trying to get them loaded into trailers.

It was a fucking nightmare.

I know dick-all about horses but I do know if they're panicked, the last place they're gonna want to go is into a dark trailer. Especially in the middle of the night, with wind blowing heat and smoke and ash and flame at them. I saw one of them kick out—damn, it was fast—and knock a guy sideways, smack into the metal trailer door. Probably got the wind knocked out of him. Once I saw the medic get to him, I turned back to my crew.

My nose twitched, even through my gear. More than wood was burning; I could smell flesh and fur, that awful barbeque-y odor that means something has died. Gray smoke billowed in the night air, and an orange glow filled the northern sky. One of the civvies, a college-age kid in a torn tank top and shorts, aimed a garden hose at the wood. It spit uselessly at the barn's sides, no good against the raging flames.

A horrid, whinnying scream came from the barn. Everyone stopped moving for a dreadful second, then pressed on with more urgency than before. Even in the orange glow, I could see the civvie with the hose go white. "Oh, shit, that's Stacy. She just foaled tonight...." He dropped the hose and ran.

Into the barn hallway, into the flames.

Shit.

I locked down my mask and went in after him.

Fire is like a gibbering boogeyman. It'll slip away behind a wall, teasing you, letting you think it's gone, then jump out like a horror movie monster, mouth open, ready to eat you. Flames lick up a wall, roaring, loud; a growling, thick sound like no other. For folks who don't know fire, it can stop them dead in their tracks with terror.

The kid didn't stop; he wavered in the smoke and heat, but he kept moving. He stopped at a stall three doors down from the active flames. "Hey, Mamacita, hey, hey, it's all right," he crooned to whatever was inside.

He rolled the stall door open just as I stepped up to him. "Sir, you've got to get out of here. Right now." Most civvies follow my orders, fire or no. I've got some size to me, and the authority to bark a little when necessary. This kid didn't even look at me. Ballsy. Or stupid.

The frantic mare rocked over a tiny foal inside her stall, tail snapping, eyes ugly wide. Her back legs were covered with blood, her tail was wet with fluids. The hay beneath them was still damp. The baby was unable to walk yet, curled at her feet. They could make it, with help.

A gust of flames blew in and latched on to the kid's shirt. I slapped it dead. The kid looked up at me, his eyes wide and desperate and blue. So blue. "Please help me. Please."

The mare screamed again. She bared her teeth, ears back as we moved, her eyes rolling with terror. She looked huge to me, her head big and flailing. The foal, curled in one corner, was still. Unconscious?

The kid went to the mare. She rose up on her hind legs, sharp hooves ready to defend.

"Stacy, Stacy, there, there. We're gonna help out. Give me your head, baby doll, give me your head." The kid let his voice go low, quiet. The mare stood back on four legs, twitching. He put one hand on her muzzle and bent to breathe into her nostrils. She snorted then stood still, her head lowered. Her sides were damp with sweat.

He tugged off his tank top and looped it over her eyes. "Lead her out first," he said to me. "I'll carry the foal."

"I'm not a horse person. What should I do?"

"Keep the shirt over her eyes, and put one hand on her neck. She'll go with you if she can't see the fire. Hold her mane, walk slowly, and she should stay with you." His voice broke and he took a deep breath. "Her name is Stacy."

"You go first," I ordered.

He bent and picked up the shivering foal. Yes, breathing; yes, alive.

I managed it—I don't know how, but Stacy obediently walked next to me, and we followed the kid through smoke and ash and the animal roar of the fire. We burst out of the barn. At the first whiff of fresh air, the mare broke loose from me; she whinnied and kicked out. I stepped aside too slowly and took a hit on the leg. She galloped away into the darkness.

On the safe side of the engine, the kid swooped to the ground. "Oxygen! Give us oxygen!" He set the foal down. One of the ambulance crew brought some blankets and slapped a mask on the tiny horse. Its slender legs stretched out and the kid smiled in relief.

I bent and touched his shoulder. "Is he okay?"

"I'm not sure, but we'll know soon. Thanks, man." His gaze held mine as I handed back his tank top. Firelight gleamed on his bare chest and sweaty shoulders.

"Stay here with the baby." I stood up. "Do not go back into that barn."

"I won't."

I went back to work. Team One lay down flame retardant around the barn's perimeter. Team Two concentrated on the roof, sucking up gallons of water from our pumper. I began to feel the smoke haze in the air, even through my respirator. Ignoring it, I focused on my job—and tried to forget the bare-chested kid and the foal.

By four, the fire was out. The front half of the barn was concrete stalls and only the roof had burned partly off that section. The back of the barn was wood construction, and it was pretty much gone. A few low walls, stained with burn marks, jutted up from the ground. The trees around the barn dripped water; it almost sounded like rain. I walked around the perimeter, assessing. Probably a 65 percent loss on the building. And two horses dead of smoke inhalation. They lay in their stalls; someone had covered them up with blue tarps, huge blobs in the dimness.

I supervised the crews packing up, giving some a verbal stroke, giving the new guy some pointers on handling the retardant hose. There are those who say firefighting is a thankless job, but I don't think that's true. Civvies, whose homes or asses we saved, were grateful enough. Sometimes, they clung to us on-site, crying, grabbing our hands, smacking us on the shoulders. And at least once a month, someone brought us homemade brownies or sent pizzas to the station.

A good-sized crowd of horse people had showed up as the night wore on. Some were owners; others were from a local horse rescue group. They moved the surviving horses out into the pastures or loaded them into trucks to haul them off the property.

I sent Jesse back to the station with the trucks. There was paperwork for me to fill out: the preliminary damage assessment, the man-hour estimate, and the county incident report. I grabbed my clipboard and slogged to the back barn, hoping to find a little quiet before the sun rose. I remembered seeing a picnic table next to a little corral on the west side, so I took my book light and a Coke and headed that way.

A few steps beyond the barn, my boot knocked into something heavy: one of our smaller oxygen canisters, probably discarded by one of our guys in the middle of firefighting and forgotten. I looped it over one arm.

It was dark behind the barn but a little glow from the security light back by the manure pile made the walk navigable. Passing the corral, I heard a grunt or groan or something. I stood still for a few seconds, wondering if it were an escaped horse. But it didn't sound like a horse.

There it was again: a throaty groan, definitely human. I peeked through the boards of the round corral. A figure crouched near the gate, hanging on to the sides, bent over.

"Hey, are you okay in there?" I kept my voice quiet.

No answer.

I stepped around the boards and found the gate. The latch had some kind of weird clip on it; it took me a few seconds to open it. The figure rose and turned away from me.

"Are you all right?" Now I could see his slender build and the tank top I'd given back to him hours earlier. The civvie.

"I'm fine, man, I'm okay." His voice was thick, teary.

I let the gate close behind me. Crickets chirped and an owl hooted from the woods on the north side. His breathing was still harsh. He was shook up and showing it.

"You ever been in an emergency before?" I asked.

"No," he said, still facing away from me. "Well, we had a horse break down at a show once. Does that count?" He gave a shaky laugh and turned to look at me.

I could see his face in the dim glow. His eyes were wide

and his face and neck were smudged with grime and ash and sweat. He raked a trembling hand through his gritty hair.

"You did a stupid thing going back into that barn."

"But at least Stacy's safe. And the baby." He put one palm on his forehead, eyebrows crunched together. "God, we lost two horses! Fuck!"

"But you saved most of them," I said quietly.

"Yeah, I guess we did."

"Do you have any idea how much worse it could have been? If your whole barn had been wood?"

"You're right." He stuck out one hand. "And thanks to you."

I took his hand, gave it a manly shake. "What you're feeling is just adrenaline wearing off. The shakes, that's all. And tomorrow morning, you'll probably feel like you got run over."

He moved closer to me, keeping hold of my hand. "Maybe not just adrenaline."

The eye contact is what tells you first. A full, direct gaze that says he's interested. A smoky, come-hither look that say he's horny. A heated stare that says come here and fuck me.

In the dimness, his hand on my neck startled me at first. Then his fingers moved down my arm, my heavy coat protecting me from any real touch. I moved to slide it off but he shook his head. "Leave it on."

His jeans were loose over his hips. He leaned on the fence and planted his hands on the rough boards. I tugged his slender arms up over his head and pressed him closer to the fencing. His back arched as I stroked down his torso. I went from his fingertips to his neck then down to his waist. With each stroke I pressed harder and harder until I was scratching down him. He groaned. "More."

I tugged my coat open, grabbed his hips, and jerked him

against me. I was hard and wired and dirty and sweaty and ready to go. I pulled his tank top up and over his head. "Should I blindfold you like I did that horse?"

"Yeah."

In a fast move, I wrapped the shirt over his eyes, tying it tight around his head, covering his eyes. He went rigid for a second then pushed back against me again. I reached around front to rough up against his nipples.

"You got anything?" I whispered against his ear, scrubbing my day's growth of beard over his neck.

Wanting to mark him.

"Left back pocket," he gasped. He faced the fence, arms trembling; I could feel their tremor as I stroked him.

In a few seconds, I was wrapped and ready to go. The condom was lubed, the cool wetness dribbling some on my balls. I glanced around. The corral area was still dark. I heard a few voices up toward the front of the barn but nothing back this way.

Geez, this was stupid.

But good. The kid writhed back against me, rubbing his ass on my cock, rubbing his face on my sleeves. My fingers found his nipples again and I pinched them—hard. His mouth opened and he bent backward, trying to kiss me.

"None of that," I said gruffly. "Just fucking." I slipped his jeans down his lean hips and ran my hands over his cheeks.

"More of this," he whispered. He grabbed my coat, the rubberized vinyl slick in his fingers, and pushed back against it.

I slipped my hand down, grabbed some of my coat front and fumbled toward his cock. It was awkward; the thick rubber didn't let me grip with any sureness but the kid just pushed up against my hand, groaning. I jerked him off as best I could through the coat. It didn't feel like much to me but he was loving it.

He thrust his hips up and forward, fucking my rubbery fist, gripping the fence boards. His ass was rounded and muscled, a nice piece of work. I watched him move for a few seconds and then I couldn't stand just watching anymore. "C'mere," I growled. I tugged him back with one hand while still gripping his cock—sort of—in the other.

He arched his back, practically begging me. I lined myself up and pulled his cheeks apart. The tan marks above his cheeks were visible: nice. And then I had an idea. I let go of his cock and stepped away.

"What the hell, man?" he sputtered. His voice was thick with frustration.

"Just a sec, let me try this." I bent to the ground and picked up the oxygen tank, twisting the knob. It hissed, steady enough for me to know there were still a few hits left. My spare mask was in my coat and I attached it to the nozzle.

"Hold this," I said, and handed him the tank.

"What the fuck are you doing?"

"You'll see. Just hold it up." I clasped the mask over my face, took some deep breaths, and felt the cool, oxygenated air open my lungs. My head cleared and I felt my senses get sharper. Now I saw strands of the kid's hair were white blond interspersed with light brown. Nail heads on the fencing stood out. Something small rustled in the hay on the other side of the corral.

Nothing like the big O to get you revved up.

I thumbed his ass open, lined up again, and thrust inside him. He grunted, moving forward with my thrust until his face was pressed against the fence boards. "Oh, ungh," he coughed. "Oh, yeah, right there." His voice was strained, husky with arousal.

I bent my knees and pushed up. The kid's mouth twisted, his

moan was guttural and incoherent. He was tensed and hard, his entire body rigid with desire and passion. He was tight and warm against my cock. In a few strokes we got that rhythm going: in, out, up and twist, our breathing getting deeper and harder. I stopped thrusting and held the mask up to his face. "Suck it."

Blindly, he bumped his nose on the side, then got his nose in the mask just right. I felt his chest expand as he took some deep breaths. I let him have a few, then pulled it away. "Oh, man," he said. "Oh, wow."

The fence boards creaked as I worked at him. The kid's fingers tightened on the rough wood, grasping and releasing, grasping and releasing. My rubber coat squeaked a little as I rubbed against him. I was sweating like mad, the vinyl not letting any breeze through except a little I felt on my face and neck as I fucked.

I slapped the mask on myself for a few hits. Oh, yeah, that buzz was growing in my head, bigger and louder. My cock went fiery hot; I could almost see it turning wine red with blood and arousal. The kid grabbed the mask back from me and slammed it on his face. "Now!" he cried out. His voice was fuzzy, wet through the plastic. "Oh, fuck, man, right now!" He moved back and I felt him clamp down on me, knew he was coming, felt my own come start in my spine and move down. My balls clenched upward, tightening; my cock pulsed rigid and I gushed into him, gripping his hips.

His head eased back and he dropped the tank. It rolled against my boot, heavy and cold. But I was light and warm and fiery.

Heated.

WHERE STEAM MEETS FLESH

Gerard Wozek

As unbelievable as it sounds, there isn't a single Starbucks here in Tallinn, Estonia. Despite the proliferation of luxe hotels and chandeliered dining rooms interspersed among the crumbling medieval walls and needling spires that loom above the refurbished streets of the Old Town, I can't find that iconic green and white symbol of caffeinated pleasure anywhere. The ubiquitous green mermaid, that winsome, two-tailed siren singing between the familiar circular logo on nearly every street corner back home in Chicago, is notably missing from Baltic culture.

I need that costly jolt of java to jumpstart my submerged libido today. I ache for the familiar tingle running from my belly to the base of my scrotum. I crave the prickly lift I get from either my dark-brewed espresso shots or the approach of a stout and stocky Baltic man. There are plenty of the latter here in the city of Tallinn, but I don't get much play for all the gawking and loitering I manage to do in the crowded Town Hall Square.

I linger for a while at the Café Tristan and Isolde near the entrance of the Town Hall and ponder the diluted taste of black coffee. I snack on a stale brioche and ponder my tour book's explication of the executions and floggings that frequently took place right here in this square hundreds of years ago. I catch the eye of a good-looking chap in a black overcoat and decide to trust that my experience here will be more gentle than what the medieval peasants may have endured.

Estonia, situated in Northern Europe between the Nordic countries and Russia, is the first excursion on a group package tour that will include two more Baltic stopovers in Finland and Denmark. I've come to this glacier-flattened country to do some typical sightseeing, gather snapshots of the church-steepled town skyline, and glean more about this upper region of Europe. I've got a couple of days to roam the medieval center of Tallinn's Old Town on my own, meandering about the narrow gated passages and bright pink, yellow, and sea green houses topped with terra-cotta roofs. So despite its lack of a trendy Starbucks coffee bar, I'm anxious to see what else this buzzing little tourist town has in store for me.

Yesterday I took a tour of the Tallinn Botanical Gardens on the banks of the Pirita River, and followed a slender, leather-jacketed native down a four-kilometer hiking path wending through craggy groves of oddly bent trees. A strong gust of Gulf Stream air seemed to be pushing me, urging me to follow this mesmeric stranger. I kept thinking we'd veer into the primeval Pirita valley and get a look at each other's native, zippered-up flora, but my hopes were dashed when he embraced what appeared to be his wife and a bundled baby in a stroller halfway past the shriveling cactus plants.

I had a similar experience during a saunter through the Saint Bridget convent, when I felt a young clergyman eyeing me near the stoic, late-Gothic style nunnery building next to the ruins of the ancient church's carcass. I'd steal a furtive glance at his dark pronounced features then duck behind a narrow tree trunk. But what started off as heavy eye contact in the old cemetery dissipated into mere scrutiny from this overtly curious priest. Sensing my heady pheromones, the cleric quickly genuflected in front of a crooked tomb marker and fled the scene.

Today, I'm still entirely jet-lagged. I'm referring to the dislocation of my mind after being in overseas transit for three days. I always experience a short-circuiting of ordinary cerebral functioning as a result of passing through a myriad of time zones and terminal changes. I teeter down the narrow sidewalks of Tallinn today, my legs and neck still cramped from the ten-hour insomniac's flight from the States. My joints are vaguely achy and I seem to fall forward as I walk.

Tallinn in November is damp and bitter. As I grope my way through the open market this morning, I'm thinking that besides a char-roasted, extra-strength sugared brew of coffee, what I could really use is a good soak in an old-fashioned steam bath. What better way to cross over borders than to strip off your jeans and head for the local sauna? The public steam room always seems to be the great equalizer when traveling. Being in the buff, drenched in sweat and natural salt next to other steaming men, is the perfect antidote to feeling like an outsider. Not knowing the language doesn't prevent me from making an essential contact with another man.

Sauna culture is quite popular in Tallinn. There is so much written about family sauna parties and unusual places within the Tallinn area to get a sweat, including a working sauna built right into a fire engine, several old fashioned smoke saunas made from chimneys in the nearby countryside, and even a floating sauna on a boat over a lake in the Sooma National Park. There is even a "Sauna" street and a touristy medieval "Sauna Tower" located right here in the Old Town.

While I'm vaguely curious about the slickly advertised gay sauna in the center of town called Club 69, I am choosing a more run-of-the-mill steam joint located in a dilapidated hotel on the edge of the Old Town, thinking I'll get a better gander at local customs. This monastic *hamam* is highlighted by a small painted sign above the entrance with the word SAUN displayed on the street. The building is located in an area that seems a shade grayer than the rest of town, as if thick, black soot has solidly encased the cement edifice.

I enter a narrow passage off the avenue, and then go down a flight of stairs to a dank, mildew-smelling entryway. The pasty-faced female attendant is more or less noncha-lant as I hand over my three hundred kroons. I'm handed a thin towel, more of a bedsheet actually, and a key for my storage. I'm motioned into a walled-off, dimly lit locker room where the clientele, mostly gentlemen in their fifties, rotund, hairy-chested, and oblivious to my gawking presence, chew on unlit cigar stubs and walk with their moistened towels tucked loosely around their bulging hips. I disrobe quickly, stow my street clothes and money belt in a metal bin, and head toward the dry sauna.

I've read that Estonians are great fans of the Finnish-style sauna and typically heat their sweat lodges to ninety to one hundred Celsius. By the looks of the tiny thermometer hung at the entrance of this small wood-paneled ten-seater, the temperature looks to be nearing its maximum. Reckoning that I'm clearly a novice with sauna society, I start my first Baltic sweat by loosening my towel and hunching over on the lower bench. I've been in Finnish-style saunas before, and universally throughout Europe, the code for behavior here is quiet reverence. The sweating that takes place within these dry heat rooms always appears to be a sacred act with conversations seldom taking place.

The air within this particular sauna is infused with a hint of juniper and eucalyptus that lodges in the back of my throat, giving my tonsils a strange tickle. I watch as a burly man steps forward and scoops what appears to be frothy pale ale from a metal bucket. Using a long wooden dipper, he gently pours it over the stones and breathes in deeply. The brew causes the scorching rocks to sizzle loudly and the dry heat to rapidly intensify. An aroma of warm honey beer washes over the atmosphere, and my head seems to levitate several inches off of my neck. The burly chap begins to gently beat his back with a long birch branch, hitting his thighs, distended belly, and hairy shoulders repeatedly. I'm thinking this must be part of a cultural tradition I'm unfamiliar with, or a somewhat arcane but rigorous detoxification process. When I offer a quick glance in his direction he motions for me to take the whittled stick. I decline and look away as the warm puddle of sweat forming on the plank between my legs expands.

Suddenly, I feel a sharp twinge of pain on my right shoulder blade as my sweathouse companion begins sharply beating me with the end of his birch rod. The tiny shoots of the branch sting as they scrape against my wet flesh. Without missing a beat, he rapidly moves down the length of my spine to the top of my buttocks. This odd ritual is accompanied with small grunts and nods of approval from the audience of three other sweat-drenched fellows.

Being a foreigner and unfamiliar with this custom of birch beating, somewhat kindred to a fraternity hazing, I grit my teeth and accept my initiation. I can endure only five minutes or so of this furnace whipping before I stand up, wrap my towel around my torso, and attempt a gracious thank-you to my masochistic buddy. The rotund gentlemen in the dry sauna begin to whisper in one another's ears. My husky, stick-whipping oppressor looks ruffled as I move away from the punishing whisk, push open the heavy wooden door, and head to the showers to cool the tiny welts that have begun to pop up on my moistened skin.

I'm convinced if I hadn't left earlier I might have begun to see mystical visions of Estonian folk dancers swirling about the tiny sudatory. Drenched with my own dripping sweat and gasping for air, I let the cool water of the pull shower rinse over my perspiration, and within moments I'm sufficiently chilled down and ready for a lengthy tub soak.

There are two water tubs situated near the entrance of the showers, each one roughly twenty-by-twenty feet square, roughly three feet deep, lit from within with green lamps and tiled around the edges with turquoise and sea blue fish engravings. I test the temperature of each shallow pool by dipping my hand in to sample the clear water. The more populated pool is the one with the coolest temperature. Actually, it is more of an ice bath. So I opt instead for the less popular warmer pool—

it's still chilly all and all, but at least I'm able to sustain a few minutes inside of it without severe goose bumps forming on my chest and legs.

Stripped down to my bare skin, I ease into the empty stillness of the tepid pool. Once I am submerged, two rather plump gentlemen of a distinguished age seat themselves on the seat ledge to either side of me. My narrow bony frame is all the more accentuated by the bulbous nature of their protruding bellies as they splash about the pool in what appears to be a series of haphazard underwater calisthenics. The gentleman on my right proceeds to make circular motions with his legs, bumping and nudging me for the entire episode, while the bald-headed fellow on my left pushes off the edge of the cooling pond and does miniature frog squats, moving up and down continuously, recklessly jostling his heavy frame up against my own.

Rather than remain seated and motionless, I decide to join in with the athletically inclined chaps and form a makeshift trio. Emulating what I believe to be a customary workout routine, I begin a series of leg crunches myself, raising my knees to my chest then pushing off into the frothy aquamarine glowing waters. The whole pool churns as the three of us jostle about in the heavily chlorinated water. The tussle however begins to take on a different turn when one of the fellows on my left grabs for my crotch. Without stopping his series of jumping crouches and appearing as though nothing remotely erotic is happening, he gently fondles and tugs at my groin.

Somewhat surprised by the nonchalance of the swift move and mindful that a rebuffing of his forward gesture might signify bad manners, I congenially allow for this mild groping. The splashing and bubbling disruptions on the surface of the water allow for a significant reduction of sight lines for pass-ersby and throughout the escapade, there is no indication of any carnal indiscretion occurring below. In fact, during the entire brief interlude, my companion has struck up a clipped conversation in what appears to be Russian with the fellow doing the leg twirls. Since I don't speak the language I make half attempts at following the hard syllabic edges and varied inflections of their discourse as my balls are softly cupped and fondled.

Though I've barely begun to even remotely "chub up" in the brisk pool, my nimble groper seems amply gratified with this brief, covert encounter, and after five minutes or so of frog-leaping in close proximity to me, he stands up, reaches for his towel, quickly wraps himself, and heads for the dry sauna. I take the cue to step out myself, and head in the opposite direc-tion, past the ice pool and the showers, to the glass-enclosed steam sauna.

I enter a narrow room of two or three disrobed men seated on five ascending rows of stone benches. No one speaks as the hiss of heavy wet steam fills the foggy dark enclosure. I remove my towel, take my place at the end of the row, and wait to be ensconced in the smoky tendrils of the densely clouded room. The high-pressured whoosh of the steam entering the musky room immediately calls to mind my favorite Starbucks in Chicago on Michigan Avenue. I feel at this moment that I myself am inside of an espresso machine, quickly getting a sense of what it must feel like to be that dark-roasted bean releasing its caffeine-rich brew.

It is suddenly within this pared down steam room in Tallinn that I am fully engaged in my youthful gayboy fantasies. Within moments of entering the wet vapor area, an old Falcon Studios porno from the late eighties replays in my head. I imagine a full-throttle orgy of wet limbs and elongated phalli flailing about in this dank Spartan steamer. In reality, however, everything here in this Tallinn sauna remains perfectly still except for the persistent rush of wet vapor that emanates from the far corner of the room. I breathe in deeply, surrendering to the thick, heady mist, and within a few minutes I'm completely saturated with steam.

I leave and reenter the wet sauna several times in order to shower and towel off the dampness. As I am drying off, a brisk fellow, my own age, in his late thirties or so, has taken note of my slingshot entrances and exits, and wisely sensing that I'm not a native of Tallinn, nods at me and to my surprise says in reasonable English, "Hallo."

"Good to meet you," I reply as I begin to reenter the steam room for one more skin-pore opening.

"You come here to rise too?" My newfound friend generously smiles, showing a slight gap between his two front teeth. I take note of his healthy tanned skin, brown eyes, and full moist lips as he motions me toward the far back corner of the steam room.

"Rise? Like rise and shine?"

"You know, to go up. Up in the steam?"

My new companion has a closely shaved head and a blue-black scorpion tattoo over his right shoulder blade. Across his muscled stomach the tattooed words MARE BALTICUM float over a classic ship anchor.

"You can follow me?" He opens the door and we reenter the desolate steam room.

"Of course."

His full biceps push against his wide chest. In soft-focus

frame I see a shock of dark brown armpit hair as he tosses his towel aside. He smells like cool amber. His fat tongue darts out across his thick lower lip. We say nothing, everything. His broad nose drips with sweat, a little droplet forming at the tip. I want it to fall on me, explode onto me. I want to be drenched in his perspiration, the musk emanating from his crotch, his breath.

"You would like to take a ride with a real sailorman?" My sea captain entreats me to move slightly forward.

"I would. I would ride across any sea wave with you."

There is a serpent uncurling in my belly, moving into my groin, making my balls tingle, my shaved organ stiffen. The engorged head of my rising penis brushes against his own hardening cock. I step forward slightly again in order to press my shaft onto his crotch.

"Be still for a moment." It's almost a soft plea followed by a quick intake of breath. He is extending his arms out, just slightly, as though he's absorbing my entire presence. "Just feel."

So I obey again and we consummate the moment. We ravish each other, wordlessly, without motion, without flailing limbs or searching tongues, without slippery caresses, or greasy thrusts. We bake in the steam. Levitating in the heavy wet air, we kiss without pressing our lips together. We devour one another's dripping flesh without letting our mouths go near scrotums, armpits, or warm ass crevices.

This is what every step in Tallinn has led me to, I think to myself. I know now the reason I came to this city: to recalibrate my senses, to surrender to this strong, poetic, Estonian sailor. We have stepped effortlessly into each other's genetic code, recognizing at once that we are each other's avatar.

"From Copenhagen to Finland, we're sailing together now,"

my sea captain whispers with eyes tightly shut. "Salt air and the wide-open waters. Can you smell it, see it?"

I imbibe his words, picturing a sky over an expanse of choppy blue-gray water. "I'll let you navigate then. Anywhere you want to go, I'm with you."

Time is suspended in this cavernous muggy den. I am aware at certain pulse points that we are standing at the vortex of where the heavy steam is initially blasting into the entire rectangular room. The tiny blond hairs on my arms are trembling with subtle but palpable electricity. The curling mist is nearly overpowering from this vantage, and the hiss and the heady smoke have effectively blotted out the rest of the room. Secluded and undetected by others within this vapory passage, the handsome stranger and I seem to have found our own plush, walled-off universe. I reach instinctively toward his tight muscular frame and high-haunch buttocks in the overpowering gray haze, but he holds back my extended arm and rests it gently at my side.

"No hands, just let the vapor raise you up." His coarse masculine voice cradles inside my throat as he steps very close to me, his powerful chest grazing my hardening nipples, but just barely. Our exposed wet skin flecks off heat waves back and forth onto one another. I'm vibrating within the continuous waves of the electromagnetic rays that are shooting off his hairy damp torso.

Our eyes are open now as we hold each other's gaze. Neither one of us uses his hands to touch the other, or ourselves. His generously sized member is rock hard and rapidly flexing in its swollen state. I match his quick muscled cock pumping with my own organ hitting against my belly. In unison, we flex our backs, our glutes, and our thigh muscles. Both our bodies are vibrating at a new pitch and it seems as if any moment I'll ejaculate into the thick air.

"Go slow," my sweet sailor cautions. "You want to savor it."

I've read of the Tantric practice of the kundalini energy rising though the spine as it ascends to the skull. It seems we have prolonged this orgasm for an inordinate amount of time— though time seems to hardly impinge on any of this alchemy. We breathe more rapidly now, the pleasure seems to rise from the belly to the brain in a continuous circuit of pure ecstatic energy.

"We are one ship, on one sea." My sailor closes his eyes and throws his head back into the pervasive fog. With those words, I recognize there is no need to spill my man juice out. No need to masturbate him or myself. No need to define this moment by an ordinary orgasm.

For a moment, the steam seems to move entirely through him, ascend and wend through his body, as though my partner has somehow become a translucent outline, a mere profile of a toned, sexy man filled with a sweet, soupy haze.

I am weightless for a moment, having transcended normal gravity. Then in another instant, I'm aware that I'm standing in the direct channel of the steam grate. My stiffly erect organ is still bathed in the deep wet heat. Still no mouths, no fingers, no rubbing of sweaty skin upon skin, but a euphoric rapture is filling me. An indescribable sense of elation and fulfillment.

Nearly breathless, I continue to gaze into this strange oracle, this womb of sexy warmth. I watch now as my swarthy sailor is transformed into a sea creature. I note the cresting green fin now of an elusive and alluring merman swimming back out into the mysterious Baltic ocean. I try to ride this wave, hold on to this roiling primeval furnace, and my sailor who provokes this sudden and tumultuous heat storm.

After another blast of wet heat, I can no longer feel my body. I have become buoyant, pure pulse and charged instinct. A wild, vital force of the universe. The stillpoint of Eros. I have evaporated into the wet tempest, and it feels as though I have broken into many hundreds of moisture pellets and I am falling onto the skin and curvy muscles of my cohort.

I am the soggy air that settles on his skin. The syrupy, humid atmosphere that moves into his heaving lungs. I am one with the impulse of his flickering libido, his heavy breathing, his pearl-shiny cock pressing firmly onto my own. We take this impulse of instant rapture head-on until we are both just one great thrust of motion and innate desire. There are moments when it seems I am unable to maintain my waking consciousness, and I simply surrender to the incessant heat blast and haplessly whirl into the flash of his dark skin and Neptunian stature and muscle and the shifting gray and white fog.

My partner has completely vanished in the steam. Unable to withstand this sodden blaze any longer, I am somehow able to regain my grounding; I step out of the wooly cushion of heat and stumble toward the exit. I teeter across the wet tiled floor to the icy bathing pool and linger inside its frigid zone for an indeterminable amount of time, waiting for my companion to emerge, but he doesn't. Was the sailor a sea ghost, just part of my intoxicated, heat-induced stupor?

Time elapses and I begin to sense the boundaries of my body again. I return to a normal waking consciousness and eventually I am able to somehow make my extremities move about, enough to dress and tip the attendant on my way out.

Being at the sauna is like resting underneath an oversized bivalve shell. For a few moments, I am able to ditch the monotony and tedium of the mundane world. I can forget about smog levels, frenetic tour itineraries, and crosstown traffic patterns and enter a tiled landscape where I am stripped down literally to only the essentials: air, water, steam, and men.

I leave the sauna completely satiated. I am no longer craving a Starbucks moment because I am as jazzed and as caffeinated as if I have just downed a double shot Americano. In fact, I have myself become the double shot, extra-sweetened Americano in Estonia.

I hail a taxi and head back toward the center of the Old Town near to where my hotel is. I pay the driver his Estonian kroons and wander about the simple grotto huts selling sheepskin rugs and handmade candles, still reeling from my venture into the mists. In my mind, I try and reach for my steam room cohort again, put my arms around him, and hold him closer to me, but he's all mist and cloudy vapor and boiling gusts.

I have come to realize that Tallinn has just about everything. I can eat the indigenous canned spicy fish sprats for a snack. I can buy a brightly painted duck or a keychain carved out wood from the Euro-Siberian *taiga*. I can take photos of the narrow steeples of St. Nicholas and St. Olav. I can swoon to the folksinging of the Estonian Philharmonic Chamber Choir or marvel at the domed Russian architecture of the Alexander Nevsky Cathedral.

I discover that I don't even need my imperialistic Starbucks coffeehouse transplanted here after all because I can sip and savor the original syrupy sweet Vana Tallinn coffee liqueur or take shots of the traditional Saaremaa Vodka, or nibble on the famous Kalev chocolate and get a better buzz here than I ever could back home. I can come back to that Estonian sauna in that remote part of town and locate the magical nexus where steam meets flesh and where men really can become like a sea Triton and for one souvenir moment, I can learn to breathe underwater with a handsome mythical sea god.

LOVE POTION #9

Mattilda Bernstein Sycamore

Voicemail on my cellphone: we met on bare-backcity or bareback-whatever. You had it. I wanted it. I'm calling to let you know that it finally took.

I play the message again, somehow in disbelief at this horrible world—the whole world first, and then the more specific world of guys searching out HIV infection and the scarier world of the guys who want to give it to them. And give them my number—ha ha—I'll breed him with my poz load, and then give him some hooker's cell!

It's hard to stay present in so much hopeless-ness, I mean way more than the usual despair, burning out my lungs and replacing them with air. Why lungs? Because heart would be too painful.

Blake calls; he says an eight-year-old boy set our house on fire—twice—so we're having a benefit. Rue says: I'm at the bottom of my everything right now. But I want to emphasize his illusions and finesse them into delusions. What about a ten-day land-and-sea vacation? Meanwhile, Ralowe wants to know if *The Hulk* made back all the money, or if there are warehouses full of green Oreos.

How many amps are in your breaker, how many breakers to get to your maker? I'm dressed up, Zero and I are frantically trying to hail a cab in the rain, and this guy says what do they call New Yorkers who used to dress like you in clubs? Club kids? That's right, he says—club kids. I spend the next day recovering from sleep; Ralowe says we need to start a group for people who don't do drugs, but feel strung out anyway. Benjamin and I talk about the tension between us, because she doesn't see herself as a queen; she constantly needs to tell me this.

Benjamin says: I don't identify with that culture, everyone wants me to perform that role, and it's disgusting. I think she's just in denial; she's the queeniest person I know. She says: I'm not invested in that identity in the way you are. I think about it. I realize she's right; I want her to be a queen too, because she's been around East Coast girls doing 4:00 A.M. runway; she knows that culture. I miss it.

I call my voicemail and it says I'm sorry—all three access lines are busy. Oh, shit—that's not my voicemail, it's the phone sex line. Before, she was an institution—now she's in an institution. At 4:30 P.M., I rush outside to get some sun. There isn't any. My trick says: ever since I moved into this new apartment, the cat has been throwing itself at the window. What do you mean? All of the sudden, the cat leaps off the bed and throws itself at the window.

Benjamin says: I haven't been able to sleep, whatever you have is contagious—I'm not used to this; I'm emotionally melting down. Benjamin was on the bus and this guy met her gaze, so she followed him to the Marina. When she got off the bus, she followed him further, and when he came out of a store he seemed surprised. Oh, hey, you're from the bus—see you later; I'm going to Sacramento.

Benjamin walked all the way to the beach—that's a long walk, were you wearing your platforms? She says it was okay because I came twice, but then on my way home I went to Mission News to cruise more—my whole life is tragic—drugs are ruining my life, even though I don't do them; everyone in my life is strung out on drugs.

I get in bed at 1:00 A.M. because I just can't function, everything hurts. As soon as I lie down, I'm wired—alarm clock! I get up to take pills. At 9:00 A.M., there's a pigeon dying in my wall. I make toast, and take another pill. I talk to the pigeon: I wish your friends could help you; I hope you won't be devoured by the rats.

It's the twenty-fifth anniversary of the Jonestown Massacre, and one of the cult survivors says it's hard to tell what's insanity and what's keeping people together. Ralowe wants to know if she could live on nori seaweed, just nori seaweed. She's vegan now, and trying to figure it all out. This is an actual Marines chant: blood makes the grass grow—who makes the blood flow? A trick calls, he wants to cross-dress at my place—well, that shouldn't be a problem, not like I usually do that kind of thing around here, but...

Rue says in Northern Europe, a standard treatment for Seasonal Affective Disorder is a homeopathic dose of gold, three times a year. I'll take a suitcase full of gold, skip the homeopathy, thanks. Blake is moving to SF and we're going to start a free door-to-door sleep deprivation clinic—Sleep Deprivation: You Want It, We Got It! Today, I feel like there's a piece of particle board between my eyes and my brain. My head is filled with distance. When I exit the bus at the same stop as this snooty British woman, she says from ahead of me: some days, it's just not worth it—getting out of bed, or getting on the bus. I say especially the first one, and I go into the Relax the Back store, just to see what they have. Everything's so expensive. When I get in bed, I can't sleep because everything itches again—is it the dust mites or am I allergic to sleep? I take a pill.

In the morning, I lie in bed staring at a piece of string rising off my sheet like a hook; it's shaking slightly due to the air purifier. I look at it closely from all different angles, but I can't figure out what it's trying to tell me. What are the barriers between a chainsaw and a child? Benjamin sees the London anti-Bush protests on TV; she says there was this huge effigy of Bush—like fifty feet tall—with a bomb in his hand and they toppled it; it was beautiful. You don't have a TV, she says, but maybe it'll be in tomorrow's newspaper.

I go over to Eric, Matt, and Jason's, and we watch *Circuit*, about, well—you know. This guy's a cop from Illinois and he moves to L.A.; within minutes he's smoking crystal and trying to kill a cat in a tree. There's someone in the movie making a documentary about circuit parties, there's the cop's childhood friend—a woman!—who's a comedian, there's the porn star, and there's a high-priced escort. The cop can't handle his drugs, the moviemaker hides his, the comedian cleans the house, the porn star injects Caverject into his dick to get hard, the escort can't feel. The climax is when the escort gets paid to kill the porn star with poison disguised as drugs, or pure drugs which are poison, but instead the escort takes the poison drugs himself 'cause it's his thirtieth birthday and his cheek implants are slipping. The former cop, who was in love with the escort, rushes in after the overdose, and then the guy who set it all up is confused; the cop chokes him for a while to teach him a lesson.

Afterwards, Eric talks about panic attacks—he thought someone was going to kill him—and I talk about incest flashbacks: I thought someone was going to kill me. Eric eats more vegan pie, and I taste it—it tastes delicious, but makes me shit. I think about everything that I want to do if the new herbalist helps—I want to exercise and feel better about my body, I want to go dancing and feel amazing afterwards and even the next day, I want to sleep.

At home, I wonder about queers who've never experienced tacky gay culture, and I wonder what they've missed out on. Outside, someone's honking their horn at me, and I figure it's the usual homophobia drama so I ignore it. But it's some woman screaming at me: do you know where the RR Bar is, Polk and Sutter? I say Polk and Sutter's two blocks; she says you wanna come? I get in the car; she's this super-posh tiny white woman, coked out of her mind on the best coke; I can tell it's the best coke because she's not biting her lips or anything, but her eyes are open wide to possibility. You're so cute, she says, can I buy you a drink? I'm okay. She says I don't care if you're okay, I want to buy you a drink. I walk her to the bar and we kiss goodbye; I really want a drink.

I think my apartment manager's a tweaker, because he's painting psychedelic clouds on the ceiling in the lobby, and he has the same hours as me. Lately, I can't seem to get to sleep before 5:00 A.M; then I'm struggling to get out of the house before dusk. Like today, focusing on the blue of the darkening sky while waiting for the bus and everything hurts. I do mean everything.

I hook up with someone on craigslist—have I broken my promise to myself to avoid it? But it's actually fun. He shakes when I lick his balls. Ralowe describes his first overnight: I still feel like I slept next to a trick, his breath smelled like a toilet, and all night long, he kept belching—in the morning, I had to pretend I liked him, I kept jerking him off and jerking him off, and he kept getting close to coming, but not going all the way there, and then I knew I had to suck him off. Andee says she wishes she could visit me, but I live in a fascist country. What about Germany? She says if there's any country that's done its share of soul-searching, it's Germany.

Zero and I listen to Carl Cox to find out what he does with the breakdown; Zero says there's one in every track. It's all about the pounding bass, heartbeat—oh, that fucking bass; do we have that here in San Francisco? When Carl Cox fades out, there's still some beautiful beat in the distance, waiting to take us home, sweet home to all that bang bang clang clang glory! It's Thanksgiving; on NPR there's a special about a turkey farmer who's researching what kinds of music turkeys like best. He says they like the wind whistling on the moors, and the Tibetan monks, but they don't like whale sounds. He doesn't tell us what they like when their heads are snapped off.

The building manager is vacuuming again—he just vacuumed two days ago. I use the neti pot, but my sinuses feel more clogged than ever, like my nose just stops at my head and nothing goes through. Well, pain, of course—that gets through. On Polk Street, this tall stumbling boy with glitter on his face stops me with a hug—you're so cute! He's smashed, and his friend with blond hair and the same glitter is embarrassed.

They're probably in high school, drinking cocktails out of Pepsi bottles with the spout cut off. I say you're cute too—I'm already getting hard with all the rubbing. He wants to go home with me, but he's supposed to go to a rave at the self-defense studio on Bush, which is a block away, even though they're pretending to be lost. I walk them in that direction, and the boy pushes me against the wall and we make out. He grabs my dick and says to his friend: look at this! She says you two can have anal sex all night long, but we have to go to the rave first—come on! I don't want to be another tired fag who grabs the boy and ditches his best girl friend—which is this boy's plan, I can tell—so I make him go with her. In the morning, there's glitter all over my face. I get the fancy full-spectrum seasonal affective disorder light in the mail, and at first I think what is this horrible heavy metal box? The light's fluorescent and not even that bright, how can it possibly mimic the sunshine at Noon? I sit with it anyway, and within a few minutes I get that clear, fun feeling in my head—oh, I have a new friend, he's awfully square, but he makes me feel special.

These days, I usually ask someone to carry my bag for me, so I don't hurt my hands, but on the way to see the herbalist in Berkeley, I'm all on my own. It doesn't feel too bad until later on, back home, after stopping at Socket's house where they're having a sing-a-long and I can't deal. At my house, everything burns, until I go on the Internet to look for sex—why?—and after that my wrists feel like they're going to split. I soak my hands in ice water, but then I'm hungry again so I have to cook. I run out to some boy's house two blocks away, he sucks me off, I run back to make pasta. My hands feel better, but my sinuses are ruined because the guy who sucked me off was smoking and all the windows were closed. I use the neti pot, and then everything feels clogged, the pasta is overcooked, it's 5:30 A.M. I go to bed.

Zero and I go to Millennium, since she's moving back to Provincetown. Of course I think about Jeremy—I think about Jeremy every time I go into just about any restaurant, it hits me all the sudden like, oh, I guess I still miss him. But I'm feeling the Love Potion #9, which is pomegranate and lemon juices with mystery herbs in a martini glass. The chestnut ravioli is one of the best parts, though the crunchy vegetables in the stuffed squash and the maple smoked tempeh are pretty amazing, not to mention the pickled onions that taste like oranges, and the persimmon—I've never had a persimmon before. Zero gets the chocolate dessert, and I'm already crashing from Love Potion #9.

Late night gas drama: unfortunately it happens in bed with a trick, he says did you just pass wind? Yes, darling. It's the guy who likes me to call him Daddy while he talks about raping my ass—what an exciting new idea! I have an ad out that says Ty instead of Tyler, and the photo's different—the trick says what happened to that nice little boy, now he's mean. Then he says: I think I'm falling in love with you. I say: open me a bank account.

Ralowe presents the new Sunday tea dance for men: Casual-Tea. Didn't I see you there? Speaking of casualties, there's Patrick, the trick who's called me ten times and asked me if I'd shit in his mouth. Last time I said don't call me anymore, you're too much of a tweaker mess. He said I have a great job. This time he's rented a hotel room at an SRO on Market; I get upstairs and he's yelling at someone inside the room: can't get the door open!

I end up with a crumpled twenty-dollar bill. Don't ask. Luckily, I don't have to spend it on a cab, since the 19 Polk appears out of nowhere to rescue me. I'm home just as the clock moves from 2:00 A.M. to 2:01 A.M. Then it's 4:00 A.M. and just when I've convinced myself that I was imagining the rats in my walls—it was really just the pigeons in the ceiling—I hear something gnawing. There's no way that's a pigeon. It sounds huge, like one of those cat-sized rats, just on the other side of my flimsy kitchen cabinets. The bottom cabinets are rotting away, and they don't even shut—I'm afraid the rat is going to swallow my kitchen whole, that means me too—help!

The next day, it's sunny and I actually get outside for a little bit of it, since I have to get to the chiropractor by four. Later, it's the first night in months when I have two tricks. First it's the Palomar, leopard pattern carpet and clouds painted on the ceiling. These clouds look better than the ones in my lobby. The trick tells me I won't smell the poppers while I fuck him, because he'll hold them close to his nose. Right. The next trick is the story; he's got the mirror and the razor blade out on the table.

His bed is so comfortable, I don't know how he ever gets out of it—and I tell him that, which he thinks is funny. He wants to cuddle, at first it feels forced but I relax into it once I'm giving him a soft massage and he's grabbing my thighs. When he sucks my dick, I make him do it slowly. Every time he moves his hands, I put them back where they belong: one hand under my balls, the other above my dick. Softly on the balls, really softly. I'm holding off, letting the tension build inside me until it almost isn't there anymore, and then building it back up again. When I come, it's so intense that I can't possibly open my eyes.

Well, okay—it's possible. I look out the window and into the next room; I close my eyes. He says how are you doing? I open my eyes, stare at the chandelier on the red ceiling while I lie there next to the trick, and he lets me. The chandelier is in three layers, but it's kind of simple too, and the music is a cheesy circuit mix but then the vocals fade out, and the music is just those minimal beats that I live for. I'm staring at the chandelier and breathing, wondering if somehow I got some coke through the trick's mouth. If the coke is this good, I'll never be able to stop.

I just keep staring at the chandelier and the ceiling, squinting my eyes so that light pinpoints me and I'm wondering, really wondering how I got so high. Everything is here, in this bed—in that chandelier hanging from that ceiling. Everything. Then there's a horn in the ceiling, in the music, just a tiny imitation car horn, honking over and over with the bells ringing and the beat, of course the beat, and then everything drops out. I'm waiting for what's next.

THE OPERA HOUSE

Natty Soltesz

Britt and Cody had rules, but you couldn't talk about them and they were always changing. This made things confusing.

Take cum, for example. They were trading hands not long after they first started beating off together. And though it was understood that they would try to cum at the same time, Britt had inwardly decided that getting Cody's cum on his hand was gross. So when orgasms approached, it was hands to one's self.

Then one night it wasn't. They were lying on the living room carpet jacking each other off, their heads up against the industrial cable spool they used for a coffee table and their feet dipping under the fabric flap at the bottom of the busted easy chair. Their slim naked sides collided in little electric volts of contact, but all

in all it was a typical scene at 3:00 A.M. in their shared apartment in the rural town of Groom, Pennsylvania.

There was a newly purchased and half-killed case of
Keystone beer in the fridge and a girl was being double-pene-
trated on the TV.

Then their heads turned and their lips touched, and the next
thing Britt knew Cody was making out with him. Making out
was questionable behavior, though they'd done it before—but
only because their TV was broken and they couldn't watch
porn, and making out helped Britt get hard. By some miracle of
the male animal mind, kissing had become purely functional.

But Britt's mom had bought them a new TV a week ago, so
that excuse was gone. Fortunately they'd been doing tequila
shots earlier that day and Cody had eaten the worm, so maybe
that forgave it, and Britt kissed right back as they writhed
around, fists working overtime. Cody's tongue slid softly
between Britt's lips, drawing their orgasms closer.

Thus in the space of a minute, two rules had been tested—
Britt was cumming and Cody was cumming, and it was
streaming all over their respective hands. As they broke apart
and wiped up Britt figured it wasn't the end of the world—they
were using the same crusty, bleach-spotted towel they'd been
sharing for weeks now anyway, so what was the difference?

One lazy Sunday morning not long after, Britt (who'd woken
up rock hard, having had an intense and wholly-forgotten
dream about Cody) shot a streaming rope of cum right across
the golden dusting of hair on Cody's chest. Cody (a towhead
with a big cock that more than made up for his lack of self-
confidence) started cumming too, and feeling turnabout was
fair play he arched his hips upward and blew jizz onto Britt's
bony pelvis. They'd chided each other about it afterward,

then that night did it deliberately, both of them directing their spewing cocks onto each other's bodies in a mock display of satiric maliciousness.

They progressed to eating their own loads, Britt one night throwing his legs up over his head with a bold smile and a devious look in his heavy-lidded eyes. He sent several creamy shots of cum sailing into his open mouth, some of it oozing down his sparsely stubbled face, then made a show of licking his lips. Cody was appropriately shocked and fake-appalled, but next time Britt "talked him into doing it" too. Soon they were regularly blasting in their own mouths, having drummed up some nonsense about how it was criminal to "waste it" and that chicks who spit were dumb cunts who didn't deserve their cocks anyway.

Not that any girls were banging down their door. Or that they necessarily wanted them to.

So. How had they progressed to eating each other's cum? Oral sex was a huge no-no, and admitting an interest in it would have been tantamount to gaily gadding about with a frilly pink parasol in hand.

The lame and tortured excuse for a catalyst had been Britt's drunken shit-talking about how "*My load tastes better than yours.*" What a con, they both knew it, but Cody took the bait like a good little guppy.

"Like you'd know," he said. They were standing in the kitchen, using one hand to suck down cigarettes and the other to tweak their half-hard dicks through their boxers.

"Whatever, dude. You know it tastes better if you eat, like, vegetables and shit, and I get those salads at McDonald's all the time," said Britt.

"My cum tastes fine," Cody said, dropping the butt of his cigarette in a beer can.

"So put your money where your mouth is. Or your mouth where my cock is," Britt said.

"Fuck you."

"You always scrunch up your face when you eat yours!" Britt said. By now he'd thrown a huge rod. It was exceptional when they found the language to talk about it, when they drew it out to the edge.

"That's cause I'm cumming. I'm like, overwhelmed."

"Bullshit," Britt said, and it was, all of it was, but when it led where it led—Britt acquiescing to his own challenge, licking Cody's load off of his slender stomach to compare and doing it hungrily ("How is it?" Cody asked. "Nasty," Britt said after he'd eaten every drop. "Told you."), then Britt jacking himself off and Cody sucking the cum off of Britt's fingers, one by one till they were clean—how could you deny it? It was filthy, and it was hot.

But you weren't allowed to say that. Once Cody had, and Britt shot him a withering look that dropped Cody's stomach like a stone in a well. It took a whole day of strained cohabitation before they were doing it again.

Life was momentary for Britt Laney and Cody Jackson. One moment they were smoking a joint of dirt weed they'd scraped together from errant baggies, the next they were shoving garage tools up their asses. (That was thanks to Britt, who'd broken the ass-ice after months of them doing all they could to avoid it.)

Momentary because the boys, both nineteen, were away from home for the first time and enjoying every minute of their independence.

They'd met after their first semester at VyoTech, the local technical school where they were studying to become auto mechanics. By spring they had moved into a unit in the Opera House on Market Street. The Opera House had been just that in Groom's late nineteenth-century heyday, when travel between Pittsburgh and Philadelphia had sent industry and the town's population booming. At some point the block building was gutted and sectioned off into apartments that hadn't been renovated since 1962, but who cared when you were paying $350 a month for a two-bedroom place? Not the landlords, that was for sure.

They were friends—best friends, and that was the extent to which they could admit to their relationship. They knew what faggots were and knew that they weren't faggots. There *were* faggots in town; older guys, boyfriends apparently, who owned a house on Spring Street—Clitter Schreve, their gear-head townie friend, had pointed it out.

At first Britt had thrown a lot of fag-talk around, but that ebbed, mainly because Cody didn't play up to it. Cody may have been confused but as far as he was concerned what he and Britt did was their business, and what the faggots did was theirs. As long as Britt thought the twain should never meet, he'd think the same.

It got a little tricky once they started blowing each other. It began as a natural progression from feeding each other loads of cum—Cody would sit on Britt's scrawny chest, his dick close to Britt's open lips, and it was only natural that his cockhead should bump against them. So Britt started wrapping his lips around the head of Cody's cock—made it easier to catch his cum, anyway, and it wasn't like you were chugging a cock past your gag reflex like some gutter whore.

Cody did it in turn, just like he did anything once Britt implicitly allowed it. They found it felt even better when the other used his tongue a little, nursing the head between his lips like it was a nipple or a lollipop. Then Britt went for broke and slid his mouth all the way down Cody's big dick, and it was cool, no big deal—so Cody began taking all of Britt's small one.

The rules regarding this were subtle and amorphous. It was okay to swallow a dick the whole way every once in a while, but bobbing the knob too much was suspect. Head movements were to be kept to a minimum. All of this was under the guise of eating each other's loads, so if you were using your mouth to help that along, fine. Sucking to suck it was not fine.

Their asses were the demarcation point, the event horizon. But from the beginning their buttholes were engaged, squinching and releasing so exquisitely as surges of pleasure swarmed through their bodies. The act of throwing their legs over their heads, warm holes exposed to the cool air, had been an unspoken but key element to what made the self-facials so exciting.

It happened one night after they'd been doing beer bongs in their apartment with Clitter Schreve and another townie, who both eventually left to find crank. Britt and Cody fell into an old-school joint jerk-off, stroking each other's cocks on the living room floor with big drunken smiles on their faces, the newly quiet apartment offering a giddy sense of promise and sexual release.

Cody had expected the usual—maybe some making out and then quasi-blowjobs. But Britt suddenly let go of Cody's dick and began tending to himself, intently watching the porno on the TV. Cody got worried, wondering if he'd crossed some invisible line.

But something was up—Britt was beating off and making it last, drawing it out longer and longer. Cody's back started to hurt from leaning against the couch, so he hoisted himself up on to it. That was when Britt swung his legs over his head, almost as if he'd been waiting for Cody to move, to give him an aerial view of his spread-wide ass.

"Man, I can't wait to feed myself a load, you know?" Britt said. He ran his hands up and down his back, feeling up his sinewy thighs, then his butt. Cody's tool was recharged—he could sense a boundary being tested. Britt was cupping his firm butt in his hands, and then his fingers were dipping into the brush of brown hair running down his crack toward his butt-hole. Cody had been keeping one eye on the porno for good measure, but then Britt's fingers were definitely massaging his hole, touching it in little jabs that he'd couple with a grunt. When Britt wet a finger in his mouth, it could no longer go ignored.

"Dude, what are you doing?" Cody said.

"Can't help it, man, feels too fucking good. You gotta try it."

"No way," Cody said as Britt brought the slick finger to his anus. He pressed it in. "Oh, man," he said, looking up at Cody from his contorted position. "It seriously feels amazing."

Cody thought *I'm drunk enough*, and got back down on the floor. He swung his blond-haired legs over his head, parting the thick cheeks of his hairless butt, thrilling to the feel of exposing that most sacred and profane of orifices. He wet his finger just like Britt had done and brought it to his light-pink hole.

The sensation wasn't entirely new—he'd done it surreptitiously in the shower a couple times—but doing it with Britt was immeasurably different. It was always these moments that were the hottest, when they were doing things they said they'd never do. Britt had an engine–grease stained finger pushed all the way in his butt, then two, and Cody matched him finger for finger and stroke for stroke. Their simultaneous orgasms came like thieves in the night.

And so the ass became the focus. They devoted hours to fingering themselves, then sticking anything up their butts that they could find. Sharpie markers, screwdriver handles, an empty tequila bottle. To grease up they used a bottle of Lubriderm Cody purchased for $4.99 at Groom Pharmacy down the street.

A week later Cody, risking ridicule, bought a butt plug from the highway porno store.

"What the fuck is this?" Britt said, turning it around in his hand. Cody explained it, and then they tested it out on Britt, whose enthusiasm swelled along with his cock.

"It just sticks in there, huh?" Britt said, reaching back to feel it.

One afternoon during a break between classes he took Cody out in the woods beside the shop. Yanking down his coveralls, he showed him the red disc of the plug handle pressed up against his butt. He'd kept it in all day.

Later Britt came home with a double-ended dildo, a gesture so enormously suggestive (the thing was shaped like a giant mutant veined cock) he was compelled to say, "Don't tell anybody about this." As if, as if.

Cody had more difficulty stuffing it inside himself than Britt did (all in all Britt had seemed more adept at taking things up his ass, though both pretended not to notice this). But they had many memorable sessions on the couch and on the floor, ass to ass, banging each other in the butt, working in tandem, separate but equal.

The weather started to cool. Cody left town one morning to help his brother move some gravel. When he got back Britt was gone. Several hours passed and he didn't return.

Cody tried to ignore Britt's absence, but by 5:00 A.M. it was painful and obvious. He felt weird—he was mad at Britt, but he didn't have a reason to be. He supposed he was worried about him, but that was stupid—Britt could take care of himself.

He lay on his bare mattress in the dark, ringed by dirty clothes, cigarette cellophanes, and empty beer cans. He wondered about this place he was in, the Opera House. Maybe he was lying where the auditorium had been. He imagined a woman on stage, her voice rising to the rafters and filling the space with overbearing sound, the audience taking it in with devouring ears and hungry souls.

Whatever. It was gone now. The lady underneath them was yelling at her kids. The guy next door sold heroin. Anything else was history.

Britt rolled in at noon the next day, Clitter Schreve in tow. Cody desperately wanted to ask what they'd been doing all night, but there was something about the way Clitter looked at him that made Cody go back to his room and shut the door. Britt and Clitter started hanging out a lot, sidestepping Cody like he was a pizza box they were too lazy to take to the Dumpster. Cody felt hollow.

One night he made Velveeta Shells & Cheese and offered

some to Britt, who ate sullenly at the table. Some wall had been erected between them overnight and out of nowhere Cody could see.

Afterward Britt had a beer and Cody joined him. They watched TV, talking more as the beer kicked in; then they were swigging whiskey and getting colossally fucked up. Cody was on the floor packing the bong. He dropped some weed and was picking it up when Britt kicked him over.

"Hey!" Cody said, laughing like it was playful. Britt had the ghost of a smile on his face. He kicked him down again. Cody grabbed Britt's leg and pulled him off the couch. They wrestled, drunkenly but seriously, knocking into furniture and using all of their muscle to hold each other down. Britt got Cody facedown on the floor and went for his boxers, tearing them off to expose his bare butt.

Cody felt violated. He grabbed Britt's thigh, then his waist, and flipped him over so hard he knocked the wind out of him. He pinned Britt's hands and yanked his sweatpants down. Britt's hard dick slapped against his stomach. Cody stared at it. He looked to Britt who had his head turned to the side. After a moment he reached out to stroke it, like they used to do. Britt endured a minute of this, then flipped onto his stomach.

Cody was confused, but he put a hand on Britt's ass and Britt backed up to meet it, so he kept it there. He got one dry finger inside him, and Britt was still gyrating his hips, face to the floor, silent. Cody stretched out on top of him, humping his dick against Britt's fuzzy crack, the head of it catching on his hole. Then Britt was adjusting his ass, and the head of Cody's cock went into Britt's asshole, and Britt backed up to take more, the pain of being fucked dry somehow bearable for him. Maybe even necessary.

Cody barely remembered cumming inside of Britt, but afterward he saw that Britt had cum too, seemingly without touching himself—there was a wet stain on the carpet, like a bad dog's mess.

Cody rolled off and lay on his back. He was beginning to drift off when a red bomb exploded in his face.

He opened his eyes to see Britt's fist coming at him again. Britt, who'd awoken tangled in Cody's limbs only to stumble to the kitchen and finish off the bottle of whiskey, crunched him square on the nose. Hot blood poured into Cody's mouth. He got his bearings and pushed at Britt, who toppled easily. Cody stood up, blood dripping on his socks, on Britt, who was rolling on the floor like some useless thing, waiting for Cody to kick him, punch him, fuck him—wasn't it all the same?

Cody stanched the flow of blood from his nose, wiped himself up with a T-shirt, threw a different T-shirt on his bare chest, and left.

The streets were dark, the lights on Market Street blinking yellow. He wandered, addled, until the sky started to brighten. He found himself in front of the queers' house on Spring Street. Like all the other houses it was dark and quiet. He stepped into their yard and crept through the wet grass along the side of the house. He looked into a window.

He hadn't expected to find them awake, but they were. One man was standing and one was sitting at the kitchen table. Cody had enough time to see that one of them, the smaller one, was pouring two cups of coffee, had enough time to think that they may as well be from another planet before the two men met his eyes.

A RETIRED WRITER IN THE SUN

Simon Sheppard

"Narrative coherence," said the Witch of Capri. "They all want fucking narrative coherence."

Quilty scribbled furiously. He would have brought his laptop to take notes, but he'd been warned beforehand that computers were banned within the sacred precincts of the Witch's cliff-top home. Not even a voice recorder passed muster. Perhaps it was some kind of obscure test, the Labors of Hercules for interviewers. Or maybe it was just the sadism of an old queen.

"And if there's one thing, my son, that life teaches one, it's that narrative coherence— hell, coherence of any sort—is largely an illusion, the fretful workings of a mind struggling to superimpose order on this squalid mess we call life."

That was a nice turn of phrase: "squalid mess." Quilty struggled to get it all down.

"So you would say that you didn't abandon erotic writing, that it abandoned you?"

"A neat formulation, but no. I simply realized that I could write porn till the crack of doom, and I'd still never succeed in getting it right."

"Getting what right? Never succeed? But..." The Witch of Capri was, after all, perhaps the preeminent voice in the entire history of gay erotica. Under a variety of pen names—some brutish, like "Ramm Hardin," others, like "Firbank Fiore," exuding more than a whiff of camp—he had churned out a remarkable seventy books, more or less, meanwhile maintaining a parallel, highly acclaimed career in Genuine Literature. All that was, of course, why Quilty was there to interview him.

"The ineffability of desire, my lad. Let me tell you a story." The Witch of Capri had, in fact, told a surfeit of stories over the preceding day and a half, but Quilty let him continue. His doctoral thesis, like it or not, depended on the garrulousness of an old man.

"Several years ago, I met this young man—and I mean young, he was nineteen at the time, or so he said—on the phone sex lines." The renowned Witch of Capri jacking off to phone sex? Now *that* was an image. "He was, he told me, tall, skinny, and a redhead, still living with his parents. And he had the softest, shyest, horniest voice. The first time we spoke, he came so quickly that I hadn't time to unzip myself. Subsequently, he'd phone me at odd times when his family was gone, and every time I heard his voice on the phone, I became instantly erect.

"He, for his part, became rather adept at phone sex. He would tell me what he was, or wasn't, wearing, and follow my lead, or at least say he was doing so. I would command him to get some spit on his hand and slide a finger up his ass, and in short order, he'd be making the most delightful moans. He didn't come as quickly as he had at first, either, though he still outpaced me every time. And he did have an annoying habit of hanging up as soon as he'd come, though a 'Good-bye' or 'Thank you' certainly wouldn't have been out of place.

"But that's not really the point, is it? If the redheaded boy had been a character in a story I was writing, I would have been expected to add some narrative aspect, some conclusion, some—no pun intended—climax. His parents would have walked in on him while he had his young dick in his hand. We would have arranged to meet, and would have had fabulous sex. Or he would have turned out to be fifty, bald, and fat. Or something. But none of that happened. He phoned me perhaps a dozen times, got off, hung up, and eventually ceased calling. That was all."

He sipped his gin and tonic and looked off to the horizon, where an improbably lovely sunset, freighted with metaphor, colored the late afternoon. "But the truth is that, more than a decade later, that unseen redheaded boy remains one of my erotic touchstones. After god-knows-how-many tricks in my life—I was quite a looker in my youth, but you already know that—I still desire that voice on the phone more than I've ever wanted just about anyone. And thinking about it still gets me hard." Quilty, unable to restrain himself, looked down. Sure enough, the Witch's rather awful caftan was tenting up.

The Witch of Capri finished off his G&T. "And nothing I could possibly write...well, let's just say that I retired for good reason. Shall we go in for dinner?" He rose shamelessly and, preceded by his famous erection, left the terrace.

The von Gloedenesque serving boy—he reeked of Mediterranean rough trade, and Quilty could only hope he was of age—cleared away dishes that had been licked clean of *panna cotta*, and poured fussy little glasses of port.

"I came, as you're aware, from a good deal of money, so I've been able to afford all this." With a grand sweep of his arm, the Witch indicated his surroundings, including the handsome young man. "And, really, at this stage of my life, there are only two major causes for discomfort. First, there's the inexorable passage of time, which is, you know, or at least can surmise, a bitch. And, perhaps more acutely, there's my utter inadequacy when confronted by the beauty of men...well, let's be honest, *young* men. Of course, I can easily afford to hire company. The financial aspect of such transactions might well be viewed as somehow demeaning, it's true. But when a smooth, slim twenty-year-old strips down, lies back, his lovely cock standing straight up against a jet black thicket of pubic hair, and, at my command, opens his ass to me till I can see the pink corona, glimpse the darkness within..." He sipped the port and stared into middle space.

At last Quilty, concerned the rest of the evening might be a waste, coughed gently. The Witch was brought back. "You know," he continued, "I'd bet that many of us who write dirty stories do it, at least in part, in an attempt to master lust. Not to overcome it, but to make it, through thought and word, our servant. To capture desire, quintessential desire. And in this we are damn well bound to lose.

"Ah, but what's a poor old fag with a penchant for words

to do? Become a writer like all the rest, it seems. I knew them all, of course. Tennessee, Truman, Bill Burroughs. They were not happy people. Understatement."

Quilty had been imagining the Witch staring quizzically at some young hustler with his finger up his butt. Now he was afraid that the interview had slid to an end. He had more than enough material, most likely, to use for the thesis, but...

"It all just makes me sad," the Witch concluded. "Melancholy. Sad."

Long, silent moments passed. At last, Quilty spoke up. "Thank you, sir. Thank you for your hospitality, and your time, and your...mind."

"Ah, but surely you're not leaving now?" the Witch said. "It's likely too late to take a train to the airport."

And Quilty had, in fact, planned to spend a second night in the Witch's guest room. "No, I just thought that our interviews were at an end."

"Well, I suppose they are. I've already nattered on far too long. Who knew, when I was churning out pulp paperbacks to be read by closeted, masturbating fags, that I would someday be the subject of something called Queer Studies?"

"Well, you're a great writer."

"No."

"Well, a good writer. An important writer."

"That's closer to the mark, I suppose." A wry smile. "You're rather an attractive young man. But you already know that."

Quilty was blindsided by the shift in conversation. But the Witch was right: he *did* know that.

"So you have, no doubt, been expecting I'd come on to you. More port?"

Quilty shook his head.

The Witch turned to the serving boy, who had been hovering in a corner of the whitewashed room. "You can go now," he said, "and shut the door behind you."

Quilty thought of an old, crass bumper sticker: *GAS, GRASS, OR ASS—NOBODY RIDES FOR FREE.* This was apparently a more literate version of the sentiment.

"Well, you know, I'm certainly more interested in my immortal reputation, however risible that notion may be, than in yet one more penis. I'll bid you goodnight."

Quilty didn't surprise himself too often, but at that moment, he did. "It doesn't have to be goodnight," he said. He tried to sound as insinuating as possible.

"I appreciate that. I can even get over my qualms over being a mercy fuck; after all, it's rather late in the game for me to stand upon my pride. But..."

"Narrative coherence, right? This is what I'm expected to do?" Quilty reached down for his crotch. "What some theoretical reader expects." He sounded, to his own surprise, a bit angry. He did not dare bring up, though, the story an assistant professor had told him of fucking Allen Ginsberg. "He was," the assistant prof had said, "getting old, was surely not very attractive, at least not to me. But that didn't matter, not really. Hell, I was having sex with *Allen Ginsberg.*"

The Witch of Capri was staring intently at him. "I have no idea," he said, "what you think you're up to. If you suppose that this is what I expected, a quid pro quo for the interview, then you might think again. I'm an egomaniac, yes, but I would so like to think I'm not that sleazy." He paused, as if for dramatic effect. "On the other hand, you are, as I previously made clear, a remarkably handsome young man. Worthy of a story, really, if I were still writing stories."

Quilty hadn't planned on standing up, but he rose. He hadn't planned on getting hard, either, but something about being the object of laserlike desire went straight to his cock. "I want to do this," he said.

"Well, I've come to the conclusion, I'm afraid to say, that sex is the one wild, true thing. Pray don't let me stop you."

Quilty grabbed at his hard cock through his khaki pants. The shape of the engorged shaft was clearly visible. The Witch of Capri shifted in his chair. "Perhaps I should move to a chaise longue for this?"

"Perhaps you should."

"To the terrace, then?"

"It's private out enough out there?"

"Relatively."

"And if someone should see us?"

"Fuck them," said the Witch of Capri.

The evening was warm, and, conveniently, the moon was full. From far below came a gentle sound of waves.

"Ah, time," said the Witch of Capri, his caftan hiked up high on one naked thigh. "You don't mind if I reminisce?"

That's nearly all you've been doing, Quilty thought. *That and complaining.* Which brought up, perhaps, the question of just why his hand was shoved down the front of his pants, stirring his cock back into full erection.

"The things people do with their dicks for no particular reason," said the Witch, quite as though he could read Quilty's mind. "Or for some reason that they'd rather not face. So are you going to entertain me or not?"

Quilty unbuttoned his trousers, letting them gap open, revealing well-filled, snowy white briefs.

"I remember when I was in school," the Witch said. "There was this Jewish boy, Chaim. He came from a family of refugees. Nice kid, smart. Beautiful boy, with dark, deep eyes and a Semitic nose. And I was so in love with him."

This line of chat wasn't helping Quilty's erection. He tried to focus in on his dick.

"I didn't do anything about it, of course. Different times. And I was too shy, if you can believe that. But after we'd gone off to college, we met up again one summer afternoon. He was wearing shorts—funny, but I can still remember that, even though much of last week escapes me—that showed off his thin, hairy legs."

Quilty had known someone like that, a Jewish boy he'd fucked. He thought of what that had been like, and his dick got harder. His host didn't stop talking, but it was obvious that he'd noticed—something in his eyes, a change in his tone of voice.

"We went for a walk in the countryside, down by a lake. He wordlessly stripped down, never taking his eyes from mine. His naked body was absolutely amazing. Hairy from the waist down, ass too, but otherwise totally smooth except for bushy armpits. Slim, defined torso, generous nipples. His dick was just average, really, but at the time I didn't know that, and as it got hard, it seemed just huge. I wanted to touch it so much, but I was so very afraid. Chaim turned and ran into the water, leaving me there on the shore with a hard-on in my pants. Several minutes later, after splashing around in the water—which, if I were writing a story, I'd probably describe as 'sun-dappled'—he came out, his dick soft now, and walked right over to me. Without hesitation, I got down on my knees. His was the first cock I ever sucked."

Quilty had stepped out of his sandals and let his pants fall to his ankles. He was rubbing himself through the thin cotton of his briefs. The Witch hiked up his caftan, raising it to his waist. He was naked underneath. Quilty gasped. The man's hard dick was absolutely huge, almost freakishly so.

"Take off your shirt for me," the Witch of Capri asked. Ordered?

Quilty unbuttoned his shirt and pulled it off.

"Very nice. Oh, and lose the pants, too. But keep your briefs on for a while. I like that. I should write about you and your briefs. Who knows, maybe I will."

Quilty knew that the Witch wasn't writing erotica anymore, but he found it an appealing notion nonetheless. *Immortality*, he thought. *Of a kind.* He turned around and played with his underwear-clad ass, then bent all the way over, hoping that the Witch could see the outline of his balls between his legs.

"Ah," said the Witch, "and such are the consolations of age."

Quilty couldn't decide whether he found that pretentiously self-pitying or not. He stood up straight and said, over his shoulder, "And of fame."

"And fame," the Witch agreed. Was that melancholy in his voice?

Quilty turned to face him. The older man was rubbing his fingertips gently over the underside of his gigantic cock.

"And did you see him again? Chaim?"

"That was a long time ago. Who knows, perhaps the whole story didn't even happen. I am a writer, you know. Many things that should be true, aren't." He looked directly at Quilty's crotch. "Would you like help with that?"

Quilty didn't know what to say. It would compromise his

scholarly objectivity—not that that wasn't long since blown away. And being sucked off by a famous pornographer would be something of an experience. At last, he nodded.

"Paolo!" the Witch of Capri called out, and, prompt as a literary device, the serving boy appeared. For Quilty, that was both a disappointment and a relief.

The dark boy, wearing only flimsy white drawstring pants, stood expectantly, waiting to be given his instructions. The Witch snapped his fingers and gestured toward Quilty.

Paolo walked over, stood directly in front of Quilty, and started stroking Quilty's chest, gradually working his way down to his crotch. When Quilty didn't object, Paolo knelt and began to peel down the front of Quilty's briefs.

"I think that you'll find Paolo to be a rather excellent cock-sucker," the Witch said, his fingers still trailing over his dick. "Perhaps the two of you can turn so I can see you better? A profile? Ah, that's it."

"Can I ask Paolo to strip?"

"Of course, my boy. Perhaps you'd like to suck him, as well? I'd enjoy that, I assure you."

At Quilty's terse instruction, the serving boy stood. His white pants were tented out at the crotch. He removed them to reveal a smaller-than-average uncut dick, fully hard. Quilty had him move till the two of them were just a couple of feet away from the Witch of Capri. A sudden, chilling breeze blew up. Quilty dropped to his knees and took Paolo's cock in his mouth.

"You see, Quilty," the Witch said, "there are a number of reasons I decided to conclude my erotica-writing career. But—to make a damaging confession—the major reason, really, was that I concluded that nothing I could write, no matter how accomplished, could possibly capture the beauty, yes beauty, of moments like this."

Quilty felt unaccountably proud. He took all of the small, hard dick deep into his mouth, grabbing Paolo's firm, hairy ass, pushing the cock even farther down his throat. He moved his fingers down the boy's hairy cleft, finding the heat of the slightly moist, responsive hole. The boy began to moan.

"We're trapped in our bodies, you see," the Witch continued, "and sex represents both resigned confirmation of that fact, and an attempt at liberation."

Quilty's pride turned to irritation. *Would you please shut up, you pretentious wanker*, he thought, *so I can concentrate on sucking cock?* He released Paolo's dick, reared back a bit, and looked over to the Witch of Capri. The elderly author, not now touching himself, was sitting there with, astonishingly, tears running down his cheeks. This was all, pretty clearly, more than Quilty had planned on letting himself in for.

He took his hand from Paolo's hole, got some spit on his forefinger. Going back to sucking Paolo's hard dick, he slid his finger inside the boy's ass. Paolo's muscles responded instantly, relaxing so he could get all the way inside the soft, hot hole.

"I've had sex with at least a thousand men," said the Witch of Capri, apropos of nothing. "There's nothing wrong with being greedy, is there?"

Sex is, Quilty thought later, on the plane back home, *most always a* de facto *narrative. Beginning, middle, end. Hard to get around that.*

If he had been a porn writer, as the Witch had been, he might have scripted the remainder of the incident with Paolo in one of several ways.

Paolo might, fairly obviously, have turned out to be a hungry bottom, one who got fucked in the evening breeze while his employer watched, jacking off. Quilty would have come inside the boy—sans condom, if he were being daring—and then all three would have buttoned up, perhaps with a bitchy/wise closing remark from the Witch of Capri.

In a slightly more wry vein, boyish Paolo would, lacking self-control, have had a premature orgasm, shooting gob after unexpected gob of sperm down Quilty's gullet. In that case, chances are that both Quilty and the Witch would have been unsatisfied, leaving them with blue-balls-level horny frustration and all its attendant charms.

If things had taken a melodramatic turn, the Witch might have maundered into a full-fledged crying jag. Paolo, the ever-faithful servant, would have fed the elderly author the pacifier that was his penis, and perhaps both he and Quilty would have shot their loads messily onto the Witch's ghastly caftan.

There was a wealth of other possibilities, other turnings. Paolo might, for instance, have turned out to be murderous rough trade, leaving both Quilty and the Witch of Capri sprawled lifelessly in darker-than-night pools of their own blood...though that rather obviously had not been the case.

Who knows? If metafiction were the game, then Quilty might have had no corporeal existence at all, being, rather, an invention of the Witch's still-fertile imagination.

The way things happen, Quilty saw, becomes clear only in retrospect.

Be all that as it may, the morning after *l'affaire Paolo*, Quilty had packed his notebooks into his overnight bag and made his exit. At the door, he hadn't been sure whether to shake the Witch's hand or to give him a hug. But the decision had been made for him. At the very last, the Witch of Capri had embraced him and kissed him on the lips, with an unexpected flourish of tongue. The moment lingered long enough for Quilty to perceive the swelling of the older man's cock, but no longer.

"Just remember to say, Quilty, to quote me to the effect that the current state of erotic writing is lamentable. Lamentable." And the Witch of Capri closed the door.

KNIVES

Xan West

For JD, who asked

Knives are about cold steel meeting warm flesh. Silky twisting penetration of the mind. Fear. Sharpness. Edge. Stillness. Knives are my threat. My cock. My will. They are careful control. Tease. Fuck. Balance. Knives reduce things to the basic and the simple. It is from there we build. From that space of fear. Or sensuality. Or coldness. Or sex.

My knife wants to go to those hidden vulnerable spaces where you think it will not dare to go. Your eye. Your lip. Your jugular. The tip of your nipple. The head of your cock. It's about more than fear. It's about showing you that you can't hide from me. Demanding all of you as my terrain. Opening you to my tools and my gaze. Making you vulnerable.

There comes a point, usually near the beginning of a scene, where I choose…between my teeth and my knife. My teeth release my beast. My teeth swiftly sink you into penetrating pain. My teeth put me up close reaching inside you, my cock throbbing against you. If I start with my teeth, my beast will meet your eyes and show you that you are his food. And the sadism moves fast along your flesh until he is fed, ending with welts on your skin that are licked and nipped, and feral eyes showing satisfaction.

I can start with a knife and if it's about fear, then you know that is the ride we are on, an appetizer to get us hard and bring us close, or the full long meal of it, with you continually invaded and mindfucked, startled and breathless. You feel the sharp edge slicing quickly through your skin, so quick that you know I can't possibly control it. You feel the sting of blood, and my tongue devouring every drop. I orchestrate every nuance, making you certain that I have ripped you open to eat you. My cock hardens as I feel the fear and horror course through you, and I reach my head down for another taste of them.

I can start with a knife and it's about sensuality. Revealing. Pleasure. Slowly slicing through the clothes you offer to my blade, teasing you with its sharpness, your bareness.

I can start with a knife and it's about coldness. Distance. Threat. You can see the sadism in me, and know that I could cut open a vein to watch your blood drip to the floor, simply because I would enjoy the sight of that. You meet my gaze and know that you are nothing but canvas for me to lay my blade onto. That I might excise one small chunk of you at a time for my dinner. That I will take you to the edge I want to be at, and you will be at the mercy of a creature that might decide to ride you over that edge for his own amusement.

I can start with a knife and it's about sex. Tracing lines

across your skin. Opening you. Exposing you. Aching to slide the sharp edge into you. You feel it tease you, the cold hardness of it thrust into you. Desire coursing through you, certain I am slicing steel deep inside you, ripping you open for my pleasure.

I can spend hours with a knife, sliding it along skin. Slowly shredding small holes in a ribbed white cotton undershirt. Removing wax in deliciously deliberate strokes, taking my time to play with the sensitive flesh revealed. Or I can spend minutes, binding you to the wall with my knife and my words, until you admit your desires and own how much you want what I will do to you. I can bring out a knife early in a scene, and then have you convinced that knife is opening the welts I have driven into your skin. Or I can take an edge just dull enough, and use that edge to lay welts across your flesh, in the pattern of my choosing.

Starting with a knife ups the ante. Starting with a knife means I will want to be inside you by the end. I will want to thrust into your willingness. I will want you helpless as I pound into you. I will want you writhing under me as I pierce you with pain. I will want to sink my teeth into you and taste your submission.

Knives whisper promises across skin. Knives rush heat in waves. Knives slide liquid into your mind. Knives open you. Just for me.

ABOUT THE AUTHORS

SHANE ALLISON is the proud editor of *Hot Cops: Gay Erotic Stories* and *Backdraft: Fireman Erotica*. His stories have graced the pages of *Best Gay Erotica 2007* and *2008*; *Bears: Gay Erotic Fiction*; *Best Gay Bondage Erotica*; *Best Gay Black Erotica*; and *Ultimate Gay Erotica*. When he's not sucking dick through the glory holes of public bathrooms, he's writing stories about sucking dick through the glory holes of public bathrooms.

TULSA BROWN's erotic short fiction has appeared in about twenty anthologies, including *Sex by the Book*; *Wet Nightmares, Wet Dreams*; *Best S/M Erotica*; and *Skin and Ink*. Her gay romance, *Achilles' Other Heel*, is available at www.torquerepress.com. Her stories have been runners-up for the Rauxa Prize for Erotic Literature twice—always a bridesmaid, never a bride.

VINCENT DIAMOND's short-story collection, *Rough Cut: Vincent Diamond Collected*, was published by Lethe Press in June 2008; more work appears in *Screaming Orgasms and Sex on the Beach*. Diamond's stories have appeared in *Best Gay Love Stories, Country Boys, Men of Mystery, Best Gay Romance 2007, Hot Cops*, in the e-books *Under Arrest* and *Play Ball* from Torquere Press, and online at Fishnet, Clean Sheets, and Ruthie's Club. Diamond is at work editing *Animal Attraction 2* for Torquere Press and *School Days* for Lethe Press. More info is at: www.vincentdiamond.com.

LANDON DIXON's writing credits include *Options, Beau, In Touch, Indulge, Men, Freshmen, [2], Mandate, Torso, Honcho*, and stories in the anthologies *Straight? Volume 2, Friction 7, Working Stiff, Hard Hats, Sex by the Book*, and *Ultimate Gay Erotica 2005, 2007,* and *2008*.

RYAN FIELD is a thirty-five-year-old freelance writer who lives and works in both Los Angeles, California, and New Hope, Pennsylvania. His fiction has appeared in many anthologies and collections in the past fifteen years, and most of it is based on personal experience. He is currently working on a novel.

JAMIE FREEMAN lives in North Florida. He divides his time between a day job as a corporate communicator and night-time flirtations with the muse. Whatever time remains, he devotes to reading, running, and watching old movies on late-night television. He has previously published a children's book and has a completed novel manuscript waiting patiently on the edge of his desk. He can be reached by email at JamieFreeman2@gmail.com.

BRADLEY HARRIS is the pseudonym of a journalist who lives in Brooklyn. This is his first published story. You can reach him at dannyboy143@hotmail.com.

LEE HOUCK was born in Chattanooga, TN and now lives in Queens, NY. His writing appears in several queer anthologies in the US and Australia, and his other work includes poetry, pieces for theater, and art installations. Additionally, he has worked with Jennifer Miller's Circus AMOK! for many, many seasons. You can reach him at www.LeeHouck.com.

DANIEL W. KELLY is author of the erotic horror collection *Closet Monsters: Zombied Out and Tales of Gothrotica*. His short stories have appeared in the anthologies *Manhandled*, *Dorm Porn*, *Just the Sex*, and *Bears*. His story "Woof!," featured in *Closet Monsters*, won first place in the erotic writing competition at bookpuppy.co.uk in January 2006. He is also a staff writer for Sexherald.com.

JEFF MANN's poetry, fiction, and essays have appeared in many publications, including *Rebel Yell*, *Prairie Schooner*, *Shenandoah*, *The Big Book of Erotic Ghost Stories*, *Best S/M Erotica Vol. 2*, *The Gay and Lesbian Review*, *Bear Lust*, *Best Gay Erotica 2003* and *2004*, and *Appalachian Heritage*. He has published three award-winning poetry chapbooks—*Bliss*, *Mountain Fireflies*, and *Flint Shards from Sussex*—as well as two full-length books of poetry, *Bones Washed with Wine* and

On the Tongue; a collection of personal essays, *Edge*; a novella, *Devoured*, included in *Masters of Midnight: Erotic Tales of the Vampire*; a book of poetry and memoir, *Loving Mountains, Loving Men*; and a book of short fiction, *A History of Barbed Wire*. He teaches creative writing at Virginia Tech in Blacksburg, Virginia.

JAY NEAL did break his leg a few years ago, but the only real benefit is the appearance of this sixth adventure in the *Best Gay Erotica* series. The experience was much as narrated; however, art imitates life only to a point and that point was physical therapist Marc (with a *c*). He was an invention, a mere contrivance to fill too many quiet, motionless, early morning hours spent healing. Fortunately, Neal's bear was also there to kiss away the pain. It's now been sixteen years of domestic contentment they've shared in suburban Washington, D.C. They're not married yet but it comes closer.

ROBERT PATRICK has written mostly plays, especially *Kennedy's Children*, and a novel, *Temple Slave*. He maintains a website featuring more than fifty pages of photographs from or relating to the Caffe Cino, the first Off-Off-Broadway theater and first gay theatre, starting at http://hometown.aol.com/rbrtptrck/CINOCONTENTS.html.

SIMON SHEPPARD is editor of the Lambda Award–winning *Homosex: Sixty Years of Gay Erotica* and of *Leathermen*, and the author of *In Deep: Erotic Stories; Kinkorama: Dispatches From the Front Lines of Perversion; Sex Parties 101;* and *Hotter Than Hell and Other Stories*. His work has also been published in nearly three hundred anthologies, including fourteen previous appearances in the *Best Gay Erotica* series. He writes the syndicated column "Sex Talk" and the online serial "The Dirty Boys Club," and hangs out at www.simonsheppard.com.

NATTY SOLTESZ has had stories published in *Ultimate Gay Erotica 2008* and *Best Gay Romance 2008*. He regularly publishes fiction in the magazines *Freshmen*, *Mandate*, and *Handjobs* and is a faithful contributor to the Nifty Erotic Stories Archive. He is currently at work on his first novel, *Backwoods*, from which "The Opera House" is an excerpt. He lives in Pittsburgh with his boo. Check out his website: http://www.bacteriaburger.com.

MATTILDA BERNSTEIN SYCAMORE is an insomniac with dreams. You must check out her new novel, *So Many Ways to Sleep Badly*, from which "Love Potion #9" is excerpted. Mattilda is also the author of *Pulling Taffy*, and the editor of four nonfiction anthologies, including, most recently, *Nobody Passes: Rejecting the Rules of Gender and Conformity* and an expanded second edition of *That's Revolting! Queer Strategies for Resisting Assimilation*. Oh—and Mattilda was the judge for *Best Erotica 2006*; remember that one? Mattilda loves feedback—visit her homepage and blog via www.mattildabernsteinsycamore.com.

XAN WEST is the pseudonym of a New York BDSM and sex educator and writer. Xan's work can be found in *Best S/M Erotica 2*, *Got a Minute?*, *Love at First Sting*, *Leathermen*, *Men on the Edge*, *M Is for Master*, and *Backdraft: Fireman Erotica*. Xan has a particular love for canes, biting, public sex, and good boys. Xan wants to hear from you and can be reached at xan_west@yahoo.com.

GERARD WOZEK is author of the short story collection, *Post-cards from Heartthrob Town*. His debut collection of poetry, *Dervish*, won the Gival Press Poetry Book Award. His short prose and poetry have appeared in various journals and anthologies, including *Bend Don't Shatter, Erotic Travel Tales, Rebel Yell 2, Queer Dog, The Road Within, Best Gay Erotica 1998*, and *White Crane Journal*, and online at Velvet Mafia and Blithe House Quarterly. His short film, *Dance of the Electric Moccasins*, won first place at the 2005 Potenza Film Festival in Italy. He teaches creative writing at Robert Morris College in Chicago.

LOGAN ZACHARY is an occupational therapist and mystery author living in Minneapolis, MN, where he is an avid reader and book collector. He enjoys movies, concerts, plays, and all the other cultural events that the Twin Cities have to offer. His stories can be found in *Hard Hats, Taken by Force, Boys Caught in the Act, Ride 'Em Cowboy, Service with a Smile*, and *Surfer Boys*. He can be reached at LoganZachary2002@ yahoo.com.

ABOUT THE EDITORS

RICHARD LABONTÉ lives on a small island off the coast of British Columbia with his husband Asa Liles, and makes a living editing numerous anthologies, proofreading manuscripts, reviewing queer books for Q Syndicate, and contemporary literature and nonfiction about nature and the environment for *Publishers Weekly*, and transforming technical writing into readable prose. Contact: tattyhill@gmail.com.

JAMES LEAR is the nom de plume of a prolific and acclaimed novelist. As James Lear, he is the author of *The Back Passage, Hot Valley*, and *The Palace of Varieties*. He lives in London.